NARCISSISM

BOOK ONE OF THE DARK TRIAD TRILOGY

VIOLA TEMPEST

VIOLA TEMPEST PUBLISHING

Narcissism
Book One of The Dark Triad Trilogy

© Copyright 2024 Viola Tempest

Cover Design by Ann Fleur Art

CONTENTS

atalia smiled as she settled into her throne. She crossed her long legs, one over the another, her sky-blue skirt falling away from her smooth, ivory legs. The cloth split right to the hip so that her citizens could witness the glory of her limbs in full view as they knelt by her bare feet. She loved when they caressed her ankles in order to kiss the rings that adorned her toes. A show of their adoration and submission to her beauty and her will.

How had she ever lived another way? *Why* had she ever tolerated sifting through the meaningless prayers and gifts sent to God by self-serving humans? They had never recognized *her* beauty, *her* magnificence. She had been a glorified messenger and postmaster; it had been beneath her.

But God had never recognized that. None of them had. Except maybe her insufferable sisters, but she couldn't have trusted *their* judgment, either. They hadn't seen her true potential and beauty, but it didn't matter now. She had her world, and at last, she was getting the recognition she truly deserved.

It was Tithing Day. Natalia looked forward to this day more than any other since it was the time for her citizens to shower her with the love and praise she deserved. Every week, they came to her with gifts, in whatever form they could think of, to prove their undying devotion to their Angelic Goddess.

Natalia tapped her long, perfectly manicured nails upon the golden arm of her throne. Every surface in her Throne Room was a glistening, reflective surface. No matter where Natalia looked, she could see her own perfect image looking back at her. And she felt content.

She ran her tongue along her plush pink lips and blew herself a kiss, her blue eyes sparkling in the golden, mirrored walls that surrounded her. She was *perfection*. God had gotten it right when He'd made her, but even *He* hadn't been able to appreciate her, not really. Hadn't been able to see that she was just trying to show *His* precious humans what *true* beauty looked like.

How could those poor, frail, pathetic little insects learn to be better if they didn't have a proper role model?

Natalia had been the Archangel of Responsibility and Merciful Love; she had been the one to receive the gifts that humanity showered upon God. God had trusted her to reward the righteous and punish the sinners, to show mercy and love, even to those who didn't quite meet expectations. Yet, when she had traveled to lead these stupid humans personally, He had been disappointed in her actions and cast her out.

He had told her that she, *she*, was unworthy. God took her wings and banished her from Heaven, all because He had said she was too vain, that she thought only of herself and not others. That she wasn't *angelic* enough.

She had never understood that; how could she not be angelic enough? He had made her, He had sculpted her, and she was the perfect version of what an angel should be. Such fools were Him and the rest of Heaven if they were too short-sighted to see the sheer immensity of her presence.

Sending her down to Earth had been the best thing He could do, especially when He'd sent her sisters after her. As much as Natalia could not tolerate them, it had amused her to see them on Earth alongside her. God had underestimated their powers, and had forgotten how perfect *she* was. They had split the Earth in three, forging worlds all of their own where God had no say in how they ran it.

Natalia could *finally* run it as the world was meant to be, where the citizens could bask in all of her glory and strive to be like her. For was she not the most glorious thing they had ever laid their eyes upon?

Of course, she was. And that was *exactly* why they spent every waking minute of their lives surrounded by her image, to remind them just how lucky they were that she had chosen *them* to be a part of her world. Only the most beautiful, the strongest, and most perfect beings could grace her world. As if Natalia would allow anything to mar the flawless utopia that she had carved out for them.

Her world was nothing like the foul mud-heap that God had created. It was a shining beacon of splendor that her citizens could be proud to call *home*. There was no poverty here because there was no need for money. The only thing Natalia's people needed to do was revere her, to spend their days creating gifts for the weekly tithe to show her how much they loved her.

She was a merciful leader. The gifts didn't need to be lavish, though of course, that won her people points if they were. All she needed was for them to prove their reverence for the one who had given them this wonderful life. She was happy enough with songs, poems, or even dances. It didn't matter what they brought, so long as she was at the center of it all. What better muse was there than the most transcendent being in all of existence?

Natalia smiled as she leaned against her throne, tilting her head back so that she could see the two carved, golden wings studded with diamonds that sprouted from her back. She may have lost her own wings, but they had been dull in comparison to the ones her artisans had created upon her throne. These were far more fitting for her.

With a flick of her hands, Natalia opened the colossal golden doors at the far end of the Throne Room. There, her citizens waited, and Natalia giggled excitedly, her heart swelling at the thought of what her people might have made for her this time. She never grew tired of their praise; why in God's name would she?

Biting her bottom lip, Natalia watched as her citizens began to trail into the Throne Room. There was a revered hush that fell over them as they made their way toward her, their heads bowed as they dared not to look upon her beauty. She could be too blinding for their tiny human hearts, she knew that; to be in the presence of sheer excellence was too much for their mortal minds to comprehend.

It only fueled her, only made her hungry for more. Those stolen glances they shot her way, the gasps of fear and ecstasy as they looked upon her flawless visage and saw all that they could never be.

Her people were led forward by her priests and

priestesses. Her most devout followers, the ones who truly saw the vision she had for the world she'd created for them, and helped the others become appreciative of her also.

"My illustrious, impeccable, exquisiteness. We bring to you our gifts, that we might bask in your faultlessness and learn to be better. May our gifts grant us your forgiveness for our own flaws in the presence of one who is flawless." Head Priest, Jules, gushed as he fell to his knees at the base of her throne. He shuffled forward on all fours, his forehead scraping along the golden floors as he gently took hold of one of Natalia's feet and kissed her toes.

"Forgiven, Jules, as you always are. Let me see what you have all brought for me," Natalia cooed, kicked him off her foot, and smiled as she watched him scurry away. She caught him sneaking a glance at her and smirked as she heard him sigh with pleasure.

The priest ushered the first of her citizens along so that they could present her with her gifts, and Natalia sat back against her throne, eager to receive them.

"Most beautiful and wondrous, I bring you wings to replace the ones taken from you," one man whispered as he lied at her feet, his arms raised with his gift.

Natalia gasped at the sight of what he'd brought for her. Attached to leather straps were wings that almost mirrored the ones on her throne. The feathers were made from delicate, filigree gold inlaid with hundreds of tiny diamonds to make them truly shine.

Now she had new wings, and they were far grander than anything *God* had ever blessed her with.

The area behind Natalia's throne was piled high with the myriad of things her people had given to her. Jewelry, art, poems, stories, songs. Anything that they could think of that might show her their loyalty. A few had even baked for her, a new concept, but one that she had found amusing, nonetheless. She could eat, though she didn't need to. Angels didn't need sustenance in the same fashion that mortals did.

Though she was intrigued to try out some of the things that they had brought her, regardless. To see whether they had made a real effort to make them exquisite enough to be worthy of passing her lips.

However, none of the gifts quite caught her attention like the handmade wings had. *That* gift remained right by her feet, and she found herself glancing at them regularly, taken by the workmanship and clear love that had gone into it.

The light had begun to fade outside her palace, and the last crowd of her people made their way toward her. While one woman sang Natalia's praises, the fallen angel took a moment to cast her gaze upon the rest gathered around, waiting for their turn. Would she see jealousy on their faces at their fellow's musical talents? Or worry that what they had to offer was not enough?

Most looked away when they caught her eyes upon them, their heads immediately bowed in reverence. Except for two. In the center of the crowd, a man and a woman were looking at each *other* in a way reserved *only* for Natalia. Her eyes grew wide at the sight of the pair, her heart racing painfully in her chest as a red mist began to form in her head.

She had been merciful to these insects, had given them the perfect home where they could have anything they wanted. Where they would never even *die*. Wasn't that what every human had ever asked for? Immortality? The ability to stave off death? Well, she had *given* them that, and all she had ever asked for in exchange was their love, their devotion, their adulation! They were here to worship *her*. They had no need to look to one another, because no one else could compare to what *she* was!

Natalia caught sight of herself on the polished surface of the floor and immediately forced herself to calm down. She refused to allow these pathetic fools to create wrinkles on her smooth skin from scowling. She would speak with Jules and ensure that someone had an eye on the pair. They would soon remember where their priorities laid... and if they didn't, well, she would deal with them then. Wouldn't she?

Just like she'd done in the past. Though she really had thought her people had learnt that lesson.

The rest of her gifts felt tainted after that, and she found it difficult not to make some snide comment to the man and woman when they came to offer her their respective gifts. She had to remind herself to keep calm, for now, and just keep an eye on them. They would face her wrath if necessary, but it really would be a waste if she were forced to end their existence. The man was *pretty.*

As the last of her worshippers handed over his portrait of her, Natalia clicked her fingers at Jules, dismissing everyone else with a wave of her hand. She watched her citizens as they hurried from her presence, their heads down as they strode back into the city. Natalia could not help but keep her eyes fixed on the pair who had dared to look at one another in her presence. If they had been vying for her attention, that would have been one thing, but she knew that look. She was experienced enough to see *desire* and recognize it.

"Illustrious Mistress, it is an honor to be alone in your presence. How can this flawed one be of service?" Jules simpered at her, cupping one of her feet in his hands.

"Look up, Jules," Natalia hissed, all her rage in her tone as she reached over and roughly grasped the man's face so that he was forced to look at her. She kept a grip on his chin as she snapped his head around, pointing at the man and woman who had lingered at the back of the group. Their hands touched briefly, and Natalia saw the way they reached out to grasp the other's little finger, her anger rising exponentially at the sight.

"*Them!*" she snarled, the sweet honeyed tone she usually used around her priest now gone. "I am perfection, Jules. I am *everything.* Yet, I can see what they are up to. They do not worship me, Jules; they are blasphemers!" She continued, flicking her hand and throwing him to the floor as she stood up, her bare feet silent as she stepped onto the cold, golden floor. "I want them watched; I want to know exactly what they are up to. I will *not* have them forget their position; do you hear me? How could they look at one another rather than at me? There is *nothing* that either has that I do not have. I am *better*."

"Lady of Perfection! I shall have my people keep an eye on them, and they will be reminded of their place. They are deluded, lost in your beauty, no doubt. How could they not be? I am blinded whenever I am in your presence."

"And your eyes have never strayed to another, have they, Jules?" Natalia asked, looming over her priest.

"Never!" the man replied in a panic, though he didn't move away from her.

"Good. Maybe a sermon or two will remind them of their obligations to me. Let us assume it is a slip in their judgment, a misstep in their desire to have me while knowing that will never be obtainable." She sighed, flicking her loose dark curls over her shoulder, letting them cascade down her back.

Natalia glanced at herself in the reflection of her throne and smiled. She reached up and caressed her own face, her heart lightened as she looked upon her own image. Silently, she chided herself for getting angry, as if those fools would want anyone other than her. Look at her! Even the word *perfect* wasn't good enough to describe her majesty.

She turned back to Jules and knelt beside the loyal priest. Natalia reached out to cup his face with her hands, lifting his head more gently this time with her long, elegant fingers as she smiled at him. Her face smiled back at her in his watery blue eyes as he began to weep at her closeness.

"My loyal priest. Remind my people of how lucky they are. I picked them from all of humanity so that they might live in the opulence of my world. They get to be in my presence and walk in my shadow so that they might better themselves. God never gave you the time, but *I* am here for all of you, in person. Send some of your acolytes to put my gifts in the vault with the rest of the tithe, and keep an eye on that pair for me," she whispered, leaning over to brush her lips against his cheek.

Jules shivered at her touch, and all but melted in her hands as he threw himself to the floor and wailed that he was not worthy, his voice reverberating around the empty Throne Room as Natalia stood up and laughed. Her giggle was a beautiful melody, like a well-composed song. She looked down at her priest as he threw himself upon her feet.

"No, Jules, you *aren't* worthy. But you *are* loyal. Go now, send your acolytes, and do as I ask." She sighed, pulling her feet from his grasp as she strode out of the Throne Room and down the mirrored corridor into the palace proper.

Natalia leaned against the railing of the balcony outside her bedroom, surveying her city. When she and her sisters had been banished, they had split the Earth into three separate realms. Small, compared to what they had been as a whole, but their *own*.

Natalia's was naturally far better than the ones her sisters had created. A shining beacon of beauty, where everything was made from gold and diamonds or polished mirrors. On every corner, her citizens could look upon statues carved in her image, so that even if they were not in her presence physically, they always had her with them. Reminding them of how lucky they were to be a part of her world.

Every human in her care resided in her perfectly polished city. The lamplight setting the buildings aglow during the night, blotting out even the stars. As if stars could even compete with anything that *she* had designed herself. Nothing was more stunning than what she had managed to create here. Her sisters liked to *think* their worlds could compare, but there was no competition in Natalia's eyes. No matter what jibes her ridiculous siblings sent across the void on occasion.

Most of the time, the world was silent, and she was free of their nonsense. Their interference grew less and less as they desperately strived to contend with what she had achieved in no time at all. As if either of them had ever had the talent to challenge her. They weren't nearly as adept at building a world as she was, a fact she had gleefully told them any time they did dare to contact her.

Oh, how grateful she was to be separated from them, and from Heaven. Here, she could create her paradise, just as it should have been. God had been a fool, just as her siblings were. He may have created her, but she could tell that He was jealous of her potential, of just how amazing He'd made her. She could challenge Him; that had been the problem, and she knew it. That was why He'd forced her from Heaven. Whatever, in the end, she was victorious, and look at all that she had achieved!

Natalia smiled as she watched the crisp, clear water spout from one of the many fountains in the city. Tiny diamonds cascading over the golden statue of herself holding her arms wide to embrace her people. To give them a glimpse of her brilliance.

Most of the city had gone to bed, though a few of her people still gathered in the glistening streets, their voices drifting lazily on the cool night air to her balcony. She couldn't quite hear what they were saying, though their tones were soft and full of love, so she assumed they were discussing her. Tithing Day really *was* what they looked forward to the most, given how they could bathe in her greatness. In person, no less.

In the back of her mind, the man and woman still bothered her. It was like a knife to her heart, seeing them look at one another that way. Natalia grinned and bit her bottom lip as a plan formed in her mind. She had asked Jules to deal with them, but she could do it so much better. They had slipped, that was all, a momentary blip in their loyalty due to their longing to be with her, to be like her. Maybe she would give them a taste, just a little, do them the honor of allowing them a glimpse of her.

"Acolyte!" she called, turning away from the balcony.

The blue chiffon nightgown she wore swirled around her silken skin, barely covering her slender, curvaceous frame, given how it was all but transparent. She had no shame; why would she? She loved to look upon herself as much as her people did, and why would she deny them a peek at her?

A young woman hurried into her bed chamber, blushing bright red as her eyes flickered over Natalia's all but naked frame. The girl threw herself to the floor, her forehead pressed against the cold, golden floor, eyes closed tight. Natalia smiled. How sweet, the poor girl didn't dare allow herself a proper look, even with the reflection on the floor.

"You called for me, my Lady of Brilliance," the girl whispered.

"Seek out Head Priest, Jules. Tell him I want to see the man that he and I discussed earlier. Tell Jules to bring the man here to my bedchamber," Natalia ordered, tapping the girl with her foot. "Hurry now."

"Yes, my Lady of Glorious Perfection!" the Acolyte replied, kissing Natalia on her foot before she hurried backwards, still not daring to open her eyes until she was almost out of the room.

Natalia sighed contentedly and moved to the huge four poster bed that dominated her room, collapsing onto the soft, marshmallow-like mattress and staring at herself in the mirror above the bed. Why she hadn't thought of this before, she had no idea.

The passage of time meant very little to Natalia as she stared at herself; after all, it was her favorite activity. She could never grow tired of looking at her curves, or the way her curls fell around her shoulders. She loved how blue her eyes were in the dim lamplight, glistening like diamonds freshly cleaned in a cool, clear river.

A knock on the door heralded the arrival of her guest, and Natalia grinned as she sat up, leaning her head on her hand while she looked at the door.

"Come in!" she called.

The mirrored door swung open, and the man from the tithe was pushed into the room roughly by the acolytes. Natalia smirked as she saw the pair glare at the man as they shut the door behind him. They knew what he was here for, even if he might not, and they hated him for the reward coming his way.

"Don't be shy. You may approach," Natalia cooed at the man, swinging herself upright. Her legs dangled over the edge of the bed, the chiffon rising to reveal her legs—not that the material really covered them, anyway. "What's your name?"

"Adam," he replied, barely looking up from the floor as he shuffled his way slowly toward the bed.

"Adam," Natalia repeated, enjoying the sweet irony in his name. How Biblical.

She looked him up and down, enjoying the look of him. He was tall and muscular, lightly tanned with light brown hair that was clearly well-maintained. Short enough to stay out of his face, but with enough length that she would be able to get her fingers through it. Like all of her people, he was good-looking.

Natalia and her sisters had picked their citizens, and Natalia had ensured that all of the best-looking humans had been brought to her world. She hadn't given her siblings much choice in the matter, and it wasn't like they could have argued with her, anyway.

Slowly, Natalia got up from the bed, moving with purpose toward Adam, watching his deep brown eyes in the reflection of the floor as he gazed at her legs from there. She stopped in front of him, and lifted his face with her fingertips, forcing him to look at her.

"Do you find me beautiful, Adam?" she asked, already knowing the answer.

"Y-yes!" he replied quickly as he stepped back, taken by surprise at the question.

"What about me do you find beautiful?" she continued, striding around him, her fingers brushing against his collarbone as she let her eyes take in his figure.

"You're perfect… your skin is flawless, pale like quality ivory with the slightest golden glow that blinds you when the sunlight hits it. Your eyes—oh gosh, your eyes—are the deepest pools of blue that see into my soul." He whimpered as she appeared in front of him again, those very eyes fixed on his, glinting back at her from his brown orbs.

Natalia smiled. "Go on," she whispered huskily, her hands on her hips as she pushed out her chest, watching the effect that she had on him.

He let out a soft, guttural growl, and she knew she had him. There was no resisting her because there was no one better than her. Impulsively, he reached out, his fingers hesitating just millimeters from her as he trembled, too afraid to let himself touch the sheer perfection of her frame. Natalia smirked, grasped his hand, and pulled him against her, her arms around his neck as she pressed her lips to his.

Adam responded to her touch without any further prompting, and Natalia let him indulge his urges without complaint. He carried her to the bed, and she enjoyed watching him devour her in the mirror, her skin flushed against his touch to give her the rosy hint she loved to see upon her body. Adam was inconsequential, just another lover to amuse herself with while she watched her own wondrous form in the mirror. He would forget the other woman now, because now, he'd touched Heaven itself.

The acolytes had retrieved Adam from her bed while Natalia slept, much as they did with any of the other lovers she deemed worthy enough to sleep with at the time. Natalia enjoyed taking a lover; it allowed her a chance to see herself in a different way—hence the mirror over her bed—and it gave her citizens something to strive for with their gifts. In the hopes that, maybe, she would call upon *them* to her bed chamber.

Natalia was confident that Adam's priorities would now be reset. He'd had a chance to experience *real* pleasure, and there was nothing that the woman she'd seen him making eyes at during the tithe could offer him now. Nothing.

She'd had female lovers on occasion, and it was an interesting experience that she would no doubt indulge herself in again at some point. Natalia was sure that Adam would go back to whomever the woman was, brimming with his newfound confidence, and dismiss her entirely. Then the woman would remember where *her* love should really be placed.

Shifting in her bed, Natalia indulged herself in her own reflection, just as she did most mornings. Exploring every inch of her skin with her eyes and hands. She tutted at the red marks that Adam had made on her pale skin where he'd forgotten himself in his desperation to touch her. They'd go quickly enough, but she hated how they looked on her usually pristine skin. No matter, she would cover them with some of the clothing and jewelry her people had brought for the tithe.

She sighed as she finally dragged her eyes away from her form. She would go and entertain herself in the vault; it was only right that she spent some proper time admiring the things that her citizens had made for her. After seeing Adam and that woman making eyes at one another, she had allowed herself to become distracted from her last gifts, and she wanted to pay them proper attention. That, and she wanted her *wings*.

Natalia smiled at that thought. She didn't need real wings when she had that magnificent pair. They were so much better than the pure white, boring, feathered ones she'd been created with.

As she pulled on a sparkling dress that hugged her curves —slitted up both sides all the way to her hips to reveal those long slender stems of pure ivory beauty—she stared at herself in the mirror, glancing at the place her wings should have been. It had been so long since they'd been there that she couldn't really remember how they had looked. They couldn't have been all that impressive, though. If they had, she would have felt *something* at their absence. But she didn't feel anything. Lighter maybe, but there was no longing or regret when she looked at her wingless reflection.

Natalia blew herself a kiss as she twirled in front of the mirror. Taking in every angle of herself before she gave herself a nod of approval. Had she ever *not* approved of herself? No. Of course not. Every outfit she chose was handpicked to accentuate her attributes. Hugging every curve, boosting her bust, and emphasizing the sweet peach that were her buttocks.

She strode across the bedroom and threw open the colossal door, smirking as the acolytes that loitered in the hallway, guarding her room, gasped and fell to the floor.

Jules' followers were as devout as they came. The man had been a priest for God before her fall from grace and the subsequent split of the world. Natalia had always thought it was such a waste, that a man as pretty as Jules had taken a vow of celibacy. Then again, the entire ideal of celibacy had seemed utterly ridiculous to Natalia anyway. Why give humans the pleasure of attraction to one another if you were then going to tell a select bunch of them that being together was a bad thing?

Merciful. God wasn't merciful. He was a hypocrite! Natalia had been loyal; she'd been devout; she'd done her duty. He just didn't like it when she'd pushed back against him. He'd made her too gorgeous, too perfect, and He had resented her for that! He always had to have what *He* wanted; why couldn't she have the same? It wasn't as if their morals were all that far removed from one another… not really.

Natalia snorted, flicking her hair over her shoulder as she strode down the corridor toward her vaults. Her image flashed at her from the corner of her eyes. Long, pale legs reflected back at her with each stride, the mirrors caressing her every movement.

The vault laid in the center of her palace, guarded at all times by Jules' followers. Not that Natalia worried about her people stealing anything; they knew better, and they would only be adding to the collection in a week's time, anyway. So, what was the use of taking something that would only be replaced?

The acolytes opened the doors for her, and Natalia giggled with delight at the giant mound of gleaming items that awaited her attention. All for her. The doors closed behind her, leaving Natalia with all the privacy she needed to enjoy her belongings. She was surrounded by splendor. Glinting gems and trinkets of all shapes and sizes, custom made for her enjoyment, all to prove the love that her people had for her.

Natalia had allowed the acolytes access in order to organize her presents. They had sectioned the vault, placing paintings in one space, sculptures in another. Jewelry hung on intricate stands, or in great heaps on ornate golden tables. Poems and songs and other presents all kept together, categorized for ease of access.

And there, her new favorite. The crowning glory of her collection.

Jules had obviously coordinated having a mannequin set up in order to display her new wings in all their beauty. After all, something as ornate as the wings should *never* just be placed on the floor. It had hurt enough to place them at her feet during the tithe. She really would have to reward the priest at some point. He did deserve a little more recognition than she'd given him.

Sighing softly, Natalia ran a delicate finger over the edge of the exquisite feathers, taken by the workmanship that must have gone into the piece. It couldn't have taken the man just a week; he must have kept this project a secret until it was ready for her.

They were *perfect*.

And she would be even more perfect wearing them.

Who knew how much time had passed since Natalia slipped the leather straps of the wings over her arms and tightened them in place with a strap above and below her breasts? She had lost herself to her image, as she did most days. Twirling and spinning and giggling as she sighed at her reflection in the mirrored walls of the vault. Taken aback by *just* how perfect her new wings were.

Nothing could have suited her more. She should have been *born* with wings this magnificent. Just another point to prove how God had tried to suppress her wonder. But her citizens understood her grandeur, and this man had sought to give her a pair of wings *worthy* of her stature. She needed to see him. Anyone who could make feathers this delicate, and with such love, was worth having by her side. She needed to hear how he loved her. She could *see* it, but she wanted to listen to him as he listed the ways he thought she was impeccable.

"My Lady of Bewitchment and Wonder, I apologize for the interruption, but one of your citizens is in a terrible state outside and wishes to see you immediately," Jules spoke softly as he hurried through the doors that his acolytes opened for him. The priest skidded across the floor as he threw himself to his knees with some force.

"Oh?" Natalia turned to face her priest, unhappy at the thought of being dragged away from her things. There were still plenty of items from yesterday's tithe to indulge in.

"He has spent the morning weeping at the doors, begging to be granted an audience with your most perfect visage," Jules added.

Natalia grinned, biting her bottom lip as her heart did a somersault in her chest. It had been a while since any of her citizens had gotten themselves this worked up. Most spent the week contemplating the time they'd been given on tithe day, working on their gifts for the next week.

"Alright, I'll see him. Poor thing. Who can blame him for needing to be close to me? I'll meet him in the Throne Room; you can let him in. Oh, Jules, I want you to find the maker of my wings for me. He's done such a wonderful job, and he needs to be properly rewarded."

"It *is* the maker of the wings, my Lady of Sublime Divine Light," Jules replied, looking up at Natalia, his eyes lingering a little *too* long on her exposed thigh. Though she didn't mind, it always amused her to see Jules shiver in excitement when he looked at her that way.

"Oh, he must be eager to see me with my wings! The

finished product!" Natalia clapped happily, stepping over Jules, her dress flapping behind her with the speed of her stride. "Give me a minute or two to settle upon my throne, Jules, then you may let him in. And I want *privacy!*" she snapped, hurrying down the corridor, the wings heavy upon her back.

Natalia grinned as she saw her *new* image reflected on the walls, floors, and ceilings of her palace. Her wings shone brightly as the light glinted off the diamonds and gold. She had always been beautiful, but her new acquisition gave her a whole new glow that she had never anticipated. Maybe she would have the man make her a crown worthy of sitting atop her head. Something similar to his previous work for her that complimented her perfectly weaved locks.

Her skin flushed with excitement at that thought. An ornate crown. It amazed her that none of her citizens had ever made her such a gift before. Maybe they had not wanted to ruin her hair, since there was never a strand out of place upon her head. She didn't blame them for that, but a crown was definitely what she needed. She would make sure the wing-maker crafted her the finest coronet that had ever been produced.

Natalia settled upon her throne, dangling her legs over one of the arms so that her dress fell away to reveal them in all their glory. She knew that they were one of her best features. One of many. And she took great pride in her long, elegant limbs. She would never taint them or restrain them with pants or anything like that. They had to be free for all to gaze upon with awe and delight.

Leaning her head upon her hand, Natalia watched as Jules' acolytes hurried to open the doors to allow her guest into the Throne Room. A smile lingered on her face as the sunlight streamed into the room, glistening upon every surface until it was almost blinding. A representation of her own bedazzling brilliance, of course.

"Come forward, citizen. Head Priest, Jules, says that you are in distress. What afflicts you so? Do you not rejoice at being one of the chosen few brought into my world? One of those fortunate enough to relish in my presence?" Natalia cooed, her skin tingling with the anticipation of hearing him heap praise upon her.

"Lady of Brilliance, I could not be more overjoyed at having been chosen by the most magnificent being in all of existence. There is no one who compares, no one who could. There are no words that can describe *just* how wondrous you are, try as I have every tithe to show you *just* how much I adore you," the man whimpered, crawling toward her on his hands and knees, his voice reverberating around the empty chamber.

"Yet, was it not you who crafted my wings?" Natalia asked, reaching back with a hand to caress her feathers with her fingertips.

"It was! For my Lady of Grace and Supremacy deserves wings to match her glowing visage. Though they pale in comparison to your beauty. Nothing in existence can hope to compare with your radiance," he continued, his voice a sharp keen as though he fought against a grieving heart to say those words.

"Then be happy! You gave me wings that even God could not provide! Fear not, you can remain at my side and bask in all of my wonder. Join the acolytes, become my priest—just like Jules—and you can bathe in the splendor of my presence daily. I have a task for a man as skilled as you, but I would have you here by my side so that you might tell me every day how much you love me. Would you like that?" she whispered, swinging her legs from the arm of her throne so that she could lean forward.

She felt the wings shift their weight on her back, threatening to topple over her head as she leaned toward the wing-maker. Thankfully, the straps held, and Natalia was more than strong enough to carry their load without even blinking an eye.

The man lifted his head slowly and dragged his eyes from the floor, as though he were still afraid to look upon her. Natalia smiled and pursed her lips at him, as though she were considering a tantrum if he even dared to contemplate denying her request. As if he ever would!

Suddenly, the man was on his feet, and Natalia gasped.

Something cold and sharp pressed against her throat, and Natalia sat still, wincing as she swallowed, feeling the edge of the knife press into her skin. Her nerves set on fire, and her skin prickled as the thought of the blade cutting her sank into her mind. Even when God had torn away her wings, Natalia hadn't been afraid, but the thought of this *lowlife* marking her in any way, now that brought fear into her heart.

"I would like that more than anything. My *wonderful* Lady, but I cannot risk them taking you from me, not now. Not ever!"

Natalia took a slow, deep breath in through her nose, forcing herself to calm down. The man had one arm wrapped around her chest, his hand upon her shoulder to force her back against her throne. The wings he had so lovingly made for her—for there was no denying the devotion in each filigree feather, so tenderly crafted and put together in honor of her—pressed painfully into her shoulder blades as she sat back. His other hand held the knife to her throat. Her skin might have been ivory, but it was as soft as the skin of a peach and would cut and bruise just as easily if she resisted him.

How dare he? *How dare he?* Rage raced through every

fiber of Natalia's being, her veins blazing with her fury as she felt ready to burn everything around her. He'd been quick, but she'd been too slow. She had never even seen it coming, the glint of the knife only registering with her moments after she felt the cold steel against her skin. She would see that blade plunged hilt deep into his damn eye before the day was through.

"Why?" she hissed, her perfectly manicured fingernails scraping along the golden surface of her throne as she forced herself not to move.

"Because I cannot bear it. They talk in the dead of night when your devotees go to sleep. I've heard their whispers. Always whispering! They thought I slept, but Samuel was too busy crafting, too busy building wings for his mistress. I couldn't sleep, not until you had wings to wear, so that you might soar above this city, away from these *fiends*. But I cannot make you fly. My wings cannot help you soar above the clouds, away from harm, away from *them*."

"What are you talking about?" Natalia snapped, wincing as she felt the blade press closer to her throat. If he made even the smallest mark, she would ensure he suffered a long, slow death rather than the quick one she had originally envisioned for him.

"The one you took to bed last night. The one they call Adam. He is one of them, one of the demons who sought to harm you. But you seduced him, and the fool was heartbroken when your acolytes came for him. He couldn't cope with being taken from your side, and so he killed himself because he would never be as beautiful as you, nor would he ever feel that way again! But his friends still plot. I hear them, always plotting," Samuel continued in a hushed tone as he moved to place his cheek against Natalia's. "They want to mar my Lady's face! They want to cut her up and leave her alive so that she can be less beautiful than they.

Jealous! That's what they are! They're all jealous!" Samuel snarled angrily.

Natalia saw her chance. In his anger, Samuel had loosened his grip, and it was enough for Natalia to take advantage. Though that had only been a matter of time, as though she would allow such an insect to *actually* do her any harm!

She felt the knife move away from her throat, and Natalia's hand snapped up to grip Samuel's wrist. She twisted it hard until the man howled in pain, and she twisted it some more. The bone in his arm snapped, the sound echoing off the walls of her empty Throne Room, but she didn't stop. Natalia turned his arm again and again, but his body could not follow to relieve the pain now coursing through him. Instead, his agonized howls drowned out the sound of the continual snap of his arm as bone and sinew gave way to the pressure that Natalia put upon it. At last, she took hold of his upper arm and threw him across the chamber, his body skidding across the floor one way, the knife another.

The inner doors of her palace slammed open as her priests and priestesses hurried into the room, led by Jules, the acolytes scurrying along behind their elders.

"My Lady!" Jules squealed, hurrying across the hall toward Natalia as she strode toward Samuel.

She tore the wings off her back and cast them aside with a snarl. Her face scrunched up in disgust as she looked over the man now cowering at her feet, cradling his shattered arm against his chest.

"You talk of others plotting against me, and yet it is *you* who holds a knife to my throat?!" Natalia screamed, kicking Samuel onto his back and pressing her foot against his chest until she felt his lungs strain for breath beneath her weight.

"I could not bear the idea of them hurting you! I would rather kill you and preserve your body in its perfection than have them cut you out of spite for their own failings! They will never be as beautiful as you, not ever, not *ever*!" Samuel screamed.

Natalia snarled, pressing her foot against Samuel's throat, reveling in the feeling as his windpipe snapped. She closed her eyes and gave a soft, satisfied sigh as she twisted her foot. Her toes pushed through skin and sinew. Hot, thick blood gushing over her ankle as Samuel's head literally popped off his neck, rolling across the floor.

She wiggled her toes, sighing as she felt the blood start to coagulate upon her skin. Tacky and wet. Opening her eyes, Natalia's nose wrinkled at the thick red pool pouring from Samuel's severed neck. His dead eyes stared at her where his head had rolled away, a trail of red leading from his body to where it had stopped.

"M-my Lady?" Jules stammered, dragging Natalia back to her senses.

"Get rid of him, and find Adam. If this man was right, then you'll find him dead. It would appear that some of our citizens have forgotten their place and their love for me. I won't have it, Jules, I won't. They are supposed to *love* me!" she wailed, stomping her foot hard on the floor with a sickening slap as the blood sprayed up from around her.

Jules crept around Samuel's headless frame, his head low as he cowered before the raging form of Natalia. This was *not* how this was supposed to be! She had given these ungrateful insects *everything*, and she wouldn't stand for this.

"I will find the perpetrators, my Lady, have no fear. I shall have them punished for conspiring against you. They will be dragged to the steps and made an example of; they will be reminded of why they live such good lives. That they owe everything to you, as you say, and that their love and devotion are the *least* they can give." Jules snarled through gritted teeth as he picked up Samuel's decapitated head.

Blood dripped from the wound on his neck, tiny sickening splashes echoed in the Throne Room as silence fell amongst those gathered around Natalia.

"Bring me their names, Jules! I want to surprise them myself. I need to *see* it for myself. This fanatic could have been telling me lies in order to try and save his own skin. To justify his actions. I want to know if what he said is *true*. Then I will deal with it," she hissed.

Natalia stared at the body at her feet and let out a wail of despair. Her legs were tainted by the blood drying to her skin; it was already itchy, and she felt disgusted standing there in such a revolting state.

"Hush, hush, my Wonderous Perfection! My girls have already gone to run you a milk bath with rose petals. We will have your skin cleansed and pristine in no time; have no fear, my Lady. Jules will deal with this supposed insurrection; *we* will take care of you." Helena's soft voice spoke to Natalia, and she jolted as the Head Priestess placed her hands gently on Natalia's back and elbow, steering her away from the mess. "Acolytes, deal with the body, and clean up this mess. I will not have Lady Natalia's magnificence in the presence of this *pollution*."

Natalia took a deep breath, whimpering as she leaned her head upon Helena's shoulder, allowing the woman to cradle her as the priestess led her out of the Throne Room. She would be perfect again soon, and then she would fix whatever crack had started to form in her people. Before it became a chasm.

Helena had led Natalia to her room, gently guiding the distraught former angel to her ensuite bathroom where Helena's young priestesses had already drawn Natalia a bath.

The bathroom was a stunning display of marble and mirrors. The smooth golden-white stone had been carved in Natalia's image, surrounding the large circular bath in the center. The central statue depicted her over the bath, her hands cupping a lotus flower as fresh water poured from the petals, continually refilling her tub. Everything glistened. Bright and beautiful, and Natalia felt calmer.

The priestesses hurried to attend to her, carrying golden

bowls filled with fresh clean water and sponges. They helped her to undress, tossing aside the soiled clothes as they hand washed her legs with slow, gentle movements. Their tender caress made Natalia smile, and the heaviness weighing upon her heart lifted as steam rose around her.

"Come, my Lady, let us take proper care of you," Helena whispered, offering her hand to Natalia and leading her to the bath.

Helena was one of the oldest humans Natalia had picked. Where almost all of her citizens were young, the Head Priestess had been the odd exception. Something about her stunning sapphire-colored eyes, with flecks of green, and the slight wrinkles on Helena's handsome face had attracted Natalia greatly.

"I wear my age well," Helena had said once, and Natalia agreed. Where ordinarily, she would have balked at the idea of lines, or any sense of aging whatsoever, Natalia enjoyed Helena's older look.

Where Jules dealt with the city, preaching Natalia's greatness to the citizens and overseeing Tithing Day, Helena and her priestesses tended to Natalia directly. The priestesses loved to dote upon her, and any chance they got to physically touch her, indirectly or otherwise, made them ecstatic. Natalia reveled in their excited shivers and eager whispers whenever she graced the girls with her presence.

Natalia stepped up into the bath, humming softly in delight as the hot water kissed her skin. The milk and minerals that Helena and her girls had filled it with were silky smooth against her bare flesh. The soft scent of the roses brought a calm to Natalia's mind as she slipped into the water that rose up to her shoulders.

She lied back, her hair creating a halo above her head as she floated on the surface, her hands swirling through the water. She smiled as she felt the petals catch in the tiny whirlpools that she made, their feather-like texture brushing against her palms.

"My poor Lady has had such a fright." Helena sighed as she settled at the edge of the bath, placing a golden jar on the edge that contained the smelling sand Natalia used to cleanse her skin. "Jules better find out if those rumors are true, and be quick about it, or I'll send *my* girls to do *his* job."

"Jules will be fine, Helena. Has he not been as loyal as you since I took you all into my service?" Natalia asked, sitting up and turning to face the woman, her wet, dark curls sticking to her perfectly chiseled features.

Helena smiled and reached out to brush the curls away from Natalia's face. The older woman was the only one bold enough to touch Natalia without prompting, a fact that amused the fallen angel.

"He has, but that is out of his lust for you, not his love for you." Helena snorted, patting the side of the bath with her hands.

Natalia rolled her eyes and smiled as she lied back, flicking her hair over the side so that Helena could rub the sand into her curls and cleanse her of any potential muck left over from her fight with Samuel. Helena had made the observation about Jules' lust on several occasions, though Natalia didn't really care for the distinction. As long as the priest adored her, Natalia didn't care what capacity it fell under. Love was love, and she deserved all of it.

"Why have I not heard these rumors before?" Natalia asked, raising an eyebrow at the woman as Helena massaged her fingers into Natalia's hair. "Surely, if what Samuel said is true, there would have been *some* indication of this before now."

"Not to my knowledge, my Lady, but then again, does that not fall under Jules' list of responsibilities? Has *he* not boasted control over your citizens?" Helena added.

"*I* am in control of them, Helena," Natalia warned carefully, her tone low and dark.

"Of course, my Lady, but you know what I mean. Jules was the one who began the services, who took charge of organizing the tithe with his acolytes. It is he who says he ensures that the city properly pays their respects to you, and yet the first we hear of this issue is through the ravings of a madman?" Helena snorted again and shook her head. "He may be loyal, but are his followers?"

The thought troubled Natalia, and she scowled. Jules could be trusted, but was Helena right? Were his priests and acolytes to be fully believed? Or could *they* be keeping secrets from her?

"Don't scowl," Helena whispered, her lips brushing against Natalia's ear like a butterfly's kiss.

Natalia sighed and relaxed into Helena's sweet touch, her body light and airy as the other priestesses slipped into the bath in order to rub her body with the smelling sands, massaging her muscles to help her stay calm.

"It is probably just a rumor and nothing more. I cannot fathom how *anyone* could not love and adore you. I can understand being jealous; you are everything we cannot be, but it has never stopped me from loving you, my Lady." Helena exhaled, running her fingers through Natalia's hair to ensure that there were no knots. "The man must have been insane. His obsession with how much he loved you having driven him mad. It's a wonder we all don't lose our minds being so close to you."

"Yes… that would make sense. Poor Samuel… to love me so much that his mind snapped like a brittle twig until he saw danger in every corner. I cannot blame him for that. He worked so hard to make me the most perfect pair of wings… Oh! My wings!" Natalia wailed, slamming her hands down in the water and causing the girls bathing her to jump.

In her anger and frustration at Samuel's actions, Natalia had smashed her precious wings. All the love that he had poured into crafting every feather was now ruined.

"Oh, they were perfect! And I wanted him to make me a crown to match them!" She bawled.

"Hush, hush now!" Helena whispered, cradling Natalia's head between her hands to stop the woman from flailing in the bath. "We will find another citizen to re-make them. It will take time, but we will have them fixed and ensure that a crown is made to match them. Have no fear, my Lady, I will not see you go without the gifts that you truly deserve."

The bath was just what Natalia had needed. Helena and the other priestesses managed to fluff Natalia's ego sufficiently, and her inner calm had returned to normal. Helena was right. How could her people *not* love her? It was such a ridiculous notion! Though she did appreciate that maybe she could make some of them lose their mind, to love so fully as Samuel clearly had until his mind had broken… It was tragic. Well, she supposed it was; hardships of that kind didn't really come into Natalia's life.

Having been pampered by her priestesses, Natalia returned to her vault in order to fully enjoy the gifts her people had brought her. If they hadn't loved her, they would never have made such wonderful gifts, now would they? Of course not! It was preposterous to even think such a thing. Poor Samuel, he truly *had* lost his mind.

"M-my Lady?" Jules's voice called out to her nervously.

Natalia turned toward him and smiled. Her piteous priest, clearly worried that she was still angry following the encounter with Samuel. She opened her arms to the man and beckoned him to her, grinning as Jules hastily threw himself at her, clinging to her waist as he fell to his knees. She cradled his head and patted him gently as one might a pet, sighing softly at the pathetic creature she called her Head Priest.

"He was right, my Lady. Adam is dead. He killed himself once he returned to his house, but he's not the only one; there are others who have strayed. My acolytes saw it with their own eyes. *Images*, my Lady, not of yourself! Samuel was telling the truth."

"Someone is losing control!" Azazel's scathing tone called across the ether.

Natalia shrieked irritably in response, launching the golden plate that she had been gripping tightly across the vault. It bounced off a wall and clanged loudly as it crashed back onto the floor, spinning for a moment before finally coming to a stop.

"I am *not* losing control!" Natalia snapped, closing her eyes as she composed herself. She didn't need to let her sister rile her; it wasn't worth it!

"What else would you call one of your own people trying

to kill you? Or that others have started to sway from your rule?" Raziel asked with a sigh.

"I call it a hiccup. Anyway, you two can't talk!" Natalia hissed, kicking a pile of poetry away from her with disdain. "Doesn't your entire world spend their time plotting ways to end you, Azazel?" Natalia continued.

"They can plot all they like. They cannot best me at my own game," her sister replied.

"They spend too much time underkilling one another to be clever enough to kill her," Raziel added. "You're losing your sway, Jegudiel."

"It's Natalia now. I don't know why you two kept your names. I chose one that's far better, and more me." She snorted, sitting on the floor, her legs crossed beneath her as she smiled wickedly at an ornate mirror reflecting her own image back at her. "And how goes the search for love, Raziel? Have you found your one true heart yet?" Natalia smirked, knowing fully well that it wasn't within her sister to love anyone, no matter how hard she tried.

"Don't deflect, Sister. It's time you realized that you cannot keep your world in check, not anymore. They don't love you, and one of these days, they are all going to see past your beauty. You'll be alone then, with no one."

Natalia felt Raziel cut off their connection, and she grunted. "Clearly, I hit a nerve."

"If she had one to hit, I would agree with you. You can lie to yourself, Natalia, but not to us. You're losing your control over them. I told you when we started down this path that you would never beat me at running your own world. Humans don't want to love you; they need to fear you. It's the only way they know how to live."

"You'll have no one to rule if you have them all kill each other!" Natalia snapped.

"The strong ones will survive, and have far more of my

respect because of it. I'm merely speeding up the process of weeding out the weak ones." Azazel chortled.

Natalia huffed and rolled her eyes at her sister's words, glad that she couldn't see the smug look on Azazel's face. She didn't need to see her sister to know that it was there.

"This is *my* world; I'm not losing control of it. I won't ever lose control! You just *wait*." Natalia hissed, slapping her hands on the floor angrily.

She heard Azazel's laughter as she cut off their connection, and Natalia screamed irritably. It was rare for the sisters to talk to one another. On the occasions that they did, it always resulted in them vying for ways to annoy the others, poking at the flaws they saw in one another.

They couldn't be right. She wouldn't believe them… the problem was that Samuel had already told her as much. He had warned her of the plan to maim her. Still, an unfounded rumor for the moment, but considering the state that Jules had been in when he returned from speaking with his acolytes… Had Samuel been right about that as well?

No.

No, she refused to believe any of it. She wasn't losing control. Her people loved her; of course, they did. She was better than any of the citizens, more powerful and intelligent than her sisters, and her beauty was beyond comparison! She'd let her pathetic siblings into her head, but she knew better than that. All Natalia needed to do was remind her people of her magnificence; that was all it was.

Yes. She would leave her palace and spend time with them, surprise them by gracing them with her wonder in *their* homes rather than her own. They would welcome her into their humble abodes with open arms. It wouldn't take her long to reignite their devotion, and then she would show her sisters exactly who's the better of the three of them. *She* knew it; she would just have to make sure that *they* did, too.

Natalia sat on the edge of her balcony, watching over her city with a far calmer mind. Jules' hysteria had only put her on edge again after Samuel's attack, but Helena had been right. To even contemplate her citizens not being totally devoted to her was ridiculous. She was the embodiment of purity and perfection. It wasn't as though they had anyone else to love as much as they loved her, and why would they? No one would ever take her place, not in the hearts of her people. Believing otherwise, that was blasphemy.

She smiled to herself as she let her gaze flicker over the quiet streets. The street lamps flickered and danced off the golden walls, the mirrors sparkling as though the stars themselves had been plucked from the sky and trapped in their surfaces. She had created Heaven on Earth. No one could deny that, and no one could take that from her. She had done that because *she* was a visionary.

Movement out of the corner of her eye drew Natalia's attention to a street below her bedroom window. Natalia raised an eyebrow as she leaned over slightly, careful not to attract the attention of whoever was out so late at night.

The figure stuck to the shadows, clearly well-rehearsed in keeping out of the direct path of the lamplight, despite the reflective surface of the entire city. Natalia couldn't see their face at all, try as she might, nor could she figure out where they were going at such a late hour.

Ordinarily, the city was asleep, except for her and a few of the acolytes who ensured they were awake lest she required something of them. So, why was this person up?

The dark, niggling feeling crept back into her heart, and Natalia's skin prickled as she hurried to the other end of the balcony, losing sight of the figure as they rounded a corner. Something was going on, and she didn't like it.

S he didn't sleep that night. Her sisters' words rolled around inside her head, echoing louder and louder while she replayed the figure's furtive steps through the city. For the first time since Natalia had been banished from Heaven, she wished she had her wings. She could have followed the sneak with ease from the air without ever being detected, but she had lost sight of them before she could work out where they were headed to.

Natalia didn't want to believe her sisters; she refused to believe that they were right about her losing control. How could *she* lose control? It was absurd! She needed to see with her own eyes. She needed to walk amongst her people... but maybe it was best that they *not* realize who she was. She would only be hindered by the adulation of those who loved her, and then she couldn't prove to herself, or to her siblings, that this doubt was all nonsense.

Jules. She needed Jules.

Reaching over to her bedside table, Natalia picked up the golden bell that rested there. She took hold of the handle between her thumb and forefinger and rang it loudly. The hammer inside the dome of the bell clinking melodically against the metal. It was a sweet sound, almost as though the maker had somehow captured a birdsong into the bell itself. Sadly, what usually preceded the delicate tone was a harsh order from Natalia. Not quite as sweet as the bell.

The bedroom door opened, and a slew of acolytes hurried into the room, their hooded heads kept down in reverence to their Mistress. Behind Jules' followers came Helena's priestesses. Natalia had never really compared the two groups before; they had always just been her most devoted admirers, but now that she was really *looking* at her people, she began to see the differences.

Helena's priestesses did not cover their faces as Jules' acolytes did. They averted their eyes whenever Natalia cast a glance their way, but otherwise, they stole whatever glimpses they could of her. They were not as wary of touching her, and they showed their devotion more through their closeness to her—a reverence of a different kind to the humble acolytes. Of course, the most glaring difference was that all of Helena's followers were females, whereas Jules did not have such gender rules.

The acolytes were always by her side, ready to complete any task that she gave to them, but they seemed almost afraid to touch her. Something that always amused Natalia. They loved her wholeheartedly, but they clearly saw her as the goddess she *should* have been recognized as in Heaven.

You did not just *touch* a God. Not when you're just a mere mortal. And Jules' acolytes were balls of nervous energy whenever they were in her presence. Terrifyingly aware of how lucky they were to even be this close to her.

Both groups lowered themselves to the ground before her. The acolytes threw themselves upon the floor, lying flat with their hands above their heads, unable to look at Natalia. The priestesses were more graceful, sneaking peeks at their Mistress before they pressed their palms to the ground, their foreheads pressed to the cold, golden floor.

Ordinarily, it would have been *just* Jules' acolytes who answered her call, but Natalia had a feeling that Helena had spoken with her girls. The rivalry that Natalia had basically ignored was coming to a head, and her Head Priestess was clearly making moves to push out the Head Priest and take *his* place as Natalia's right hand. Interesting. Some of her people were making *more* of an effort, rather than less…

"I'm going into the city; I need to see with my own eyes what is going on with my own people. Since I cannot trust the word of anyone but myself," she snapped.

"My Wonderous Lady, you can trust *our* word. We would never lie to you," one of the priestesses uttered softly in response.

Natalia snarled, stomping her foot on the floor angrily. "No? Then how is it that not *one* of you has informed me of what has been going on in the city until Samuel attacked me?! The acolytes are out in the city, preaching to the others, and my priestesses swear that they are in the know, and yet, *none* of you knew?! Either you are *lying*, or you are all ignorant. Which is it?"

Silence fell in the room as Natalia loomed over the handful of devotees at her feet. Before she could say anything more, there was movement at her bedroom door, and she looked up to see Jules and Helena entering side-by-side. A united front? Or were they going to play off one another to see who could come out on top? Natalia could do with the entertainment. She could at least bask in *their* passion toward her.

"My Lady, we seek only to protect you," Helena whispered as she knelt beside her priestesses. She bowed her head as she offered her hands in apology, ready to receive her punishment if Natalia so decided that she required one.

"So, what you are saying to me is that you *knew* and chose not to tell me?" Natalia hissed.

"Oh, Beautiful Goddess sent from Heaven, we were too blinded by our love for you to see the signs within the city. It is our devotion that has made us ignorant of the actions of your people, the people *we* were assigned to guide in the ways of loving you. I take full responsibility for this, and I will do all that I can to rectify my oversight. Head Priestess, Helena, and I agreed that until we were *sure*, we would not tell you. We needed to make amends for our sins, for failing you." Jules whimpered, lying flat at her feet, his fingers trembling against her bare toes.

She had half a mind to kick him away from her. Natalia's body was positively quaking as she tried to contain her rage. They had hidden it from her, not just making excuses for not seeing the signs *before* there was a problem. She had trusted them! That was *her* mistake. Assuming that *mortals* could do anything right. If she wanted a job done correctly, she had to do it herself.

She knew that better than anyone; that was why she had built this world. To prove her point that she was the best of the angels, and that God was wrong.

Infallible. That's what He liked people to think about Him, but they were all wrong. She was prideful because she knew she was the best, and He was just too afraid to admit it.

Well, she would show Him, she would show her sisters, and she would show *all* of them!

"Fetch me one of your acolyte's robes, Jules. Helena, I want a wig. You're going to do your utmost to make me look *plain*, like all of you," Natalia growled through gritted teeth.

"M-my Illustrious and Superb Lady?" Jules stammered, his head whipping up from the floor as he dared to look at her, blinking rapidly in surprise.

"I'm going to walk amongst my people, and I'm going to see *exactly* what is going on."

elena had found her a crimson wig to wear, and helped Natalia tuck her glorious curls out of sight. The priestesses had removed her anklets and toe rings, placing socks and soft leather plimsolls over her elegant feet. It had taken Natalia a full hour to calm down the second they were on. They were restrictive, and she could already feel that they were going to leave her with blisters. Her poor, perfect feet were going to be *ruined* because her people had been so incompetent.

Helena had done all she could to calm the fury, promising that the priestesses would be ready to attend to her the moment she returned so that they could massage, pumice, and smooth out any rough skin before it formed. They would *never* allow her to have a flaw; it was unthinkable! Was her body even able to have such horrors? Of course not. No one could make a mark on beauty like that.

Seeing herself in all of her mirrors had only made her tantrum worse, her rage palpable as she stomped her feet so hard that she caused the palace to physically shake. Helena and Jules had been forced to calm her fury, reminding Natalia of *why* she was doing this, and that she did still look beautiful, regardless of her disguise—it was just a different kind of beauty.

Once she had calmed down enough, Natalia raised the hood of her robe, lowering it over her face so that she could remain as anonymous as possible when her face was plastered on every corner of the city.

With her disguise in place, Natalia joined a group of Jules' acolytes. Copying their mannerisms as the group shuffled out of the palace, Natalia joined them as they hurried into the streets to go about their business, preaching her wonder to all her citizens so that they might always bask in the glory of her existence.

How long had it been since she'd actually walked the streets that her citizens occupied? Natalia honestly couldn't remember. She had been so preoccupied with having them come to *her* that she had never thought to grace them with her magnificence.

Had that been where she'd gone wrong? Had they wept for the lack of contact with her and strayed in their desperation to fill the void that her opulent personality left when she didn't walk amongst them? Once a week with her wasn't enough; of course, it wasn't! How naïve she had been to think that her citizens would settle *just* for one day! They *needed* her. Their love had no outlet if she was not in their presence.

Distance makes the heart grow fonder. That was how the phrase went, wasn't it? She had believed that allowing them the time to make her gifts, limiting them to being with her in person once a week, would merely strengthen their adoration for her. It did, for some, but for others, they *needed* to be with her. Well, she would make sure to fix that from now on... once she had eradicated any of the false idols that Samuel had led her to believe existed.

Natalia kept her head down, peering out from beneath the hood of the robe. Her heart skipped a beat every time one of her citizens looked her way. She breathed a sigh of relief when they turned their gaze elsewhere, and Natalia grinned. Her ruse was working perfectly, but of course, it was, and had been, *her* idea. after all! The pain of looking like this would be worth it in the end, once she saw what was going on with her own eyes.

The crowds parted to allow the acolytes through the streets, and Natalia was surprised to find so many of her citizens' faces contorting as though they were disgusted to be in the presence of her preachers. Some bowed and looked on in reverence, while others grabbed at the robes of the acolytes as though some of Natalia's presence might rub off on them by proxy.

Reaching one of the many squares dotted throughout the city, the acolytes soon came to a halt on their pilgrimage, stopped by several citizens who wished to speak with them on several matters. Natalia took the opportunity to shuffle out of the main group, slipping past the preoccupied citizens toward the nearest building as the owner hurried out to see what the commotion was outside. She caught the door as it shut behind the man and slipped inside while he was busy looking at the growing mass of people out in the square. Natalia shut the door quietly behind her, lowered the hood from her face and gasped as she looked around the room that she found herself in.

"No. *No!*" She squealed, stomping her feet and clenching her hands so tightly that her nails dug deep into her palms.

It was just as Samuel had warned, and as Jules and Helena had feared to tell her. Upon the walls, where Natalia had expected an array of images depicting *her* beauty, she found pictures of another woman entirely—the woman who came into the room at that moment and looked at Natalia in terror.

"NO!" Natalia screamed, and the crowd outside silenced the moment her voice thundered from the house.

She moved like lightning. Shedding her robe onto the floor as she bolted to where the woman stood, Natalia's elegant fingers wrapped around the woman's throat so tightly that her nails tore into the offender's throat.

"Blasphemy! Treason! How *dare* you betray me like this?!" Natalia screamed, spittle flecking the face of the woman gasping under Natalia's vice-like grip, but the former archangel did not loosen her grasp. "You dare to go against my word and create these false images? Your defiance will not go unpunished!" she hissed.

The woman's eyes rolled in her head, her fingers trembling against Natalia's hand weakly as she tried to wrench the angel's digits from her throat. To no avail. Most of Natalia's powers had been lost when God had taken her wings, but not all of them, and she was still a formidable opponent. Clearly, her citizens needed to be reminded of who she was in this world.

With all her considerable might, Natalia launched the woman across the room. She smiled at her own strength as her victim flew the length of it and smashed through the wall, tumbling into the square beyond with the rubble.

Natalia sighed contentedly as she threw off her wig, bending to remove the shoes and socks from her feet. She tossed them aside gleefully, sneering at the discarded articles she loathed so much. Wiggling her toes, Natalia closed her eyes and allowed herself a moment to enjoy the renewed freedom she felt, now that her feet had been released from those prisons. Thankfully, she hadn't worn the restrictive things for too long; her feet *should* be free of any injury, at least.

Preoccupied with herself, Natalia had not registered the screams and shouts of the citizens crowded in the square beyond. She licked her lips as she stretched her neck from side-to-side, rolling her shoulders as she loosened the muscles in her back where her wings had once been. It had been such a long time since she'd last indulged in any real violence—not since Lucifer's uprising with his demon spawn, at least. Natalia had forgotten the simple pleasures that a show of her true strength could bring.

Striding across the room, she stepped through the large hole in the wall that she'd created when she tossed that piece of *filth* outside. The citizens closest to her scurried backwards, their faces devoid of color, their eyes wide as they looked upon their queen.

Now, they were beginning to remember their place. Clearly, Natalia just needed to remind them of it more often. A show of force, then. If that's what it would take, Natalia would *happily* oblige. She would obliterate every blasphemous article from her city and ensure that her people did not forget their place in this world *ever* again.

Her eyes fixed on the crumpled, bloodied mess of the woman she had cast aside, cradled in the arms of the man who exited the house before Natalia had snuck inside. She snorted at the pathetic state they were in now—the woman a shattered, broken mess in the arms of her sobbing lover. How had that man *ever* thought her worthy of a portrait in comparison to Natalia?

Natalia bolted across the square at the pair before the man could have the chance to run away, let alone react to her sudden appearance. The former archangel grabbed the man by his throat with one hand, tearing the bloodied corpse from his embrace with the other. Natalia held him up above her head, grinning as the wild image of herself reflected in the nearest building's glistening golden walls.

"You really thought I wouldn't find out about your treachery? Did you forget who rules this world? *Did you?!*" she screamed, her grip tightening, throwing the woman away just as she had done before.

The corpse hit the fountain in the center of the square with a sickening, crunching thud before splatting indignantly into the water below. Natalia cocked her head to one side, giggling as she saw the fountain water turn red as the woman's blood tainted its crystal-clear purity. That would need to be rectified, but at that moment, Natalia had to admit that red was a color that looked rather good on her. She would have to remember that, get rid of some of those pastel garbs of hers in favor of something a little bolder.

"I won't forgive you," Natalia whispered to the man as she looked up at him, relishing in the way he gasped against her hand, his legs kicking as though somehow, he might get her to loosen her grip. Just as that woman had done. It was pathetic.

Slowly, Natalia lowered the man until his feet touched the ground. She could see her own stern expression looking back at her in his eyes, her perfectly plucked eyebrows furrowed so that a line formed between them just above her nose. That wouldn't do. She couldn't allow these *peasants* to give her wrinkles!

Natalia smiled, almost sweetly, and relinquished her grip on the man's neck. He gasped and spluttered, coughing violently as he drew in deep swathes of oxygen, desperate to fill his deprived lungs. His gaze never left Natalia's as he wheezed, his eyes watering from the assault, though she could see the relief in his face at the fact that she had let him go.

Foolish man, as if that had been enough of a lesson for him and the other traitorous fools? No, no. Not yet.

There was a spark of amusement, like a pleasing electrical shock, that tickled across Natalia's skin as the man came to realize that he hadn't been let off the hook at all. He could see the same dark smile that she could see grinning back at her from every surface of her city; there was no joy in that expression, just murderous rage.

His scream was cut short when Natalia's hands shot out, grabbing his head so tightly that her knuckles turned white. The man's eyes bulged in their sockets, his cheekbones shattered, and Natalia sighed happily as she felt his skull snap under the pressure of her palms. Blood poured from the man's eyes, nose, and silently screaming mouth, his face considerably thinner than it had been before. Smiling, Natalia let go of his crushed skull, watching with disdain as his body crumpled at her feet, brain matter oozing from the remains of their broken cage onto the golden cobbles.

Natalia sighed as the screams escalated behind her, the citizens who had borne witness to their goddess' rage finally beginning to understand the severity of the crimes that had been committed by these two mutinous fools. No one insulted Natalia and got away with it. No one.

She spun about, blood spattering from her hands as she pointed at Jules, who looked as pale as the rest of the witnesses cowering under her intimidating stature.

"Find them, Jules, find them all. I want you to go through every residence and weed out the heretics. Bring every offending, blasphemous article to the palace steps, along with those who have *dared* to turn their backs on me. I will show them what their betrayal has brought them." She snarled, catching sight of the viscous red liquid already drying on her perfect alabaster skin. She let out a small squeal of panic, and the acolytes hurried to her side, gently taking her hands and wiping the blood away with their robes.

At least *they* had not forgotten their love for her. Soon, she would remind the rest of them who they should be grateful to, who *deserved* their love.

Natalia had lingered in the city while Jules' acolytes raided the remaining houses in the square, overseeing the clean-up of the courtyard and the fountain until she was satisfied that every nook and cranny had been thoroughly cleaned. She wanted every trace of the pair she'd destroyed eradicated from existence. They didn't deserve even one *skin cell* remaining in her domain. They had proved that they weren't worthy enough to be in her presence. She wasn't going to tolerate it from them or anyone else, not now, not ever.

The entire city was in turmoil. The commotion she created in the square quickly spread like wildfire to all of her citizens, until all were aware of their Mistress' rampage against those who dared to turn their gazes elsewhere. As if anyone else in this world, or any other, was even worth looking at other than Natalia herself? The entire notion was laughable. How far her people had fallen from her good graces!

Maybe Azazel was right to turn her citizens against one another for her own pleasure; it might even teach them some humility—they knew better than to turn against her, lest they lost their lives in her disgusting arenas and tournaments.

Well, now Natalia would just have to keep a tighter rein on her own citizens, wouldn't she? They only had themselves to blame. She had been more than generous with them! Not only did she *allow* them the privilege of being surrounded by her image, basking in the glory of her magnificence in whatever way they chose to do so, but she had granted them eternal life as well!

Her sisters ruled with iron fists and fear, while Natalia had granted *her* people a gift that humanity had been searching for ever since they'd had the brain cells granted to them to *think*. Humans had become obsessed with immortality from the moment they understood what mortality was, and they had gone to great lengths to stave off death. How many pointless wars had been started in the pursuit of everlasting life? Natalia had lost count centuries before her fall, laughing at the stupidity of man over something as simple as not dying.

Yet when she had created this world of hers, she had *readily* granted her people that gift. She didn't want them thinking of anyone other than herself; they didn't need to, after all. There was no one better than her. So, they didn't need to lie together to reproduce offspring in order to love her. She had hand-picked *them* because they were as close to being worthy, being close to her, as any being could be. Other than herself.

Maybe it would have been simpler to just duplicate herself, but then again, she didn't want to share her perfection in that fashion, either. She was the one true impeccable being in existence, and these foolish humans were meant to recognize that and love her for that. Most did, she knew that; of course, they did. How could they not?!

She was beginning to doubt again. Letting Samuel's words, and the jibes of her sisters, sneak into her mind and question her own faultlessness. *This* was why she kept contact with her siblings to a minimum. They had always known how to get under her skin, and even with age, the pair still managed to find a way to rile her. She was clearly tired. That's what all of this was. She wasn't losing control; she had just gotten a little complacent. *She*, Natalia, did not *lose* control. God might. Her sisters might. She did not.

Once she was satisfied that Jules and his acolytes had the situation under control, Natalia returned to her palace with a small escort. Greeted by the welcoming embrace of Helena and her priestesses, each of whom were eager to serve and please their goddess as they always were. Proof that Natalia wasn't losing her grip on her world; it really was all in her head.

Maybe she needed to start taking more lovers. She used to have one man a night come to her chamber to *physically* show his adoration of her... with the occasional woman where Natalia desired female company.

In a way, it was true that a woman knew how to please her more than a man ever could, given how they were naturally more aware of a woman's form and where pleasure could be obtained. Natalia had strayed from such pleasures— except for Adam from the other night—and had always enjoyed such things.

Complacency. *That* was what all of this was. She had become too comfortable letting her people shower her with praise once a week, and hadn't made any effort to walk amongst them, let alone give them a taste of *her* for some time. Well, it was time to let them touch ecstasy, sample perfection, and revel in her glory *personally* as they had done in the beginning. They had grown restless without her, searching for anything to fill the void in their hearts that she left when she wasn't with them. Could she *really* blame them for seeking other avenues of entertainment?

"You're scowling, my Lady, what troubles you so?" Helena asked as she ran her thumb over the spot between Natalia's eyebrows, smoothing out the small knot that had formed— one that Natalia hadn't even been aware of.

Natalia sighed, lying back in her bath, relaxing into the warm water and letting the aroma of honey and rose petals fill her lungs.

"I was just thinking. Have I been neglecting my people? Is that why this is all happening? So caught up in myself, thinking that once a week would be enough to satisfy their need for me. I don't blame them for wanting *more* of me; it's only natural. Only right. My absence has allowed them to stray, to seek alternatives that were more accessible to them because of *my* vacancy from their lives."

Helena ran her fingertips along Natalia's shoulder lazily. "My Lady is as wise as always, of course. That's all it is. Jules and I should have thought of such a thing, but of course, it's my beautiful Lady who figured out why there is so much discontentment amongst the citizens. What would you have us do to help you rectify this, my Lady?" Helena whispered, her lips brushing against Natalia's ear, sending little shivers of pleasure along the angel's spine.

Natalia smirked, looking up at Helena from under her long lashes. The woman had always been bold in her advances of Natalia, and Natalia had always allowed it since it was Helena's way of showing her adoration. She always wondered how long the Head Priestess would continue to shower her with such devotion, when Natalia never reciprocated the favor in any fashion.

Not once had she taken the priestess to bed with her, believing that the gift of herself was something she needed to keep for those less privileged than Helena and Jules. The citizens who didn't get to spend their time in her presence as the priestesses and the acolytes did. Would Helena turn against her eventually? Or would her bold advances start to drop away as Natalia continued to stay just out of the woman's reach?

No matter. For now, she held Helena's interest entirely. Until she didn't, Natalia wasn't going to worry over such things. Her priestess was loyal, and she was letting that doubt wiggle its way in again, even when she had worked out what had gone wrong, so to speak.

A knock on her bathroom door ruined the relaxing atmosphere, and she exhaled irritably. She remained as calm as she could, reminding herself that she had been scowling more and more lately. She would get wrinkles if she wasn't careful.

Helena made a soft hiss between her teeth at the other priestesses in attendance, and Natalia smirked as she imagined the Head Priestess glaring at the other girls for not immediately finding out who dared to disturb their Lady's bath. She heard the door open, and the sound of feet scurrying across the tile to one side of her bath, but she refused to open her eyes.

"Oh, Illustrious Illusion of Grandeur, we have gathered all forbidden artifacts and have them waiting for your inspection outside the palace doors, along with the owners of the offending items. They await your punishment. I had my acolytes bring the rest of the city to bear witness, so that they might learn their lesson as well," Jules whispered beside her.

"Good. I shall be out in a moment. Time to remind my people of their place before I grant them the gift of more time with me. Punishment, then reward; that should set things back into balance."

She had taken her time to get ready. Her people could wait; she was not going to rush for them because they didn't deserve it. They had upset her; they had forgotten her! If it wasn't because she realized that her own perfection had caused this disruption, she would have hidden herself away from the world for an entire week! Deprive them of her magnificence entirely.

Instead, she would punish those who had dared to stray rather than show her their devotion properly. Samuel had gone about things in the wrong fashion, but at least he had proven his admiration for her in his madness. Why couldn't they have all made more effort?

They could've spoken to Jules and the acolytes, and *they* would have informed her of how sad her people were at their lack of contact with her! How easily all of this could have been resolved without the need for such ugliness as violence and death...

They would fix this, and then she would be able to go back to normality, enjoying their attention and being worshipped as she truly deserved to be. The chiffon dress she'd chosen to wear as she graced them with her presence barely covered her exquisite frame. Loose and almost see-through it billowed around her long legs, caressing her skin like petals upon the wind. Always moving, gentle and loving.

Jules and Helena led the way through the palace, striding side-by-side, their respective followers flanking Natalia like an honored guard. She held her head high, her loose curls cascading over her shoulder as she walked, calmed by the presence of her reflection on every surface as they went toward the entrance of the palace.

Her priest and priestess threw open the ornate doors, and Natalia felt as though she had been punched in the gut at the sight of the items that Jules' acolytes had found that were *not* of her image... or about her in any fashion! A few pieces, that was all she had expected. One or two items, maybe ten, but this? This was far more than Natalia could ever have imagined.

There, the dark tendrils of doubt began to slither their way into her heart and mind again, and she felt her sisters press against the walls of their divide, eager to laugh and taunt her for her own naivety. She didn't need to hear their words to know exactly what they would say. Natalia knew she would have to let them in at some point, but she couldn't bear hearing their gloating *now* when she had to face *this*.

She strode out the doors, faced with the reality of just how many of her people had betrayed her. After all she had done for them, after everything she had *given* them? *This* was how they thanked her? By spitting in her face with these ugly objects that depicted people and things that could not remotely compare to her glorious, flawless image?

Her eyes scanned the huge pile that the acolytes had managed to collect from around the city. So much, so many. A soft buzz began to ring in Natalia's ears as the world around her became a numb blur. Her skin prickled, her nerves on fire, her heart pounding so hard in her chest that she was sure the whole city could hear it. The doubt truly had a hold of her heart now, its claws digging deep as doubt became certainty.

It wasn't a handful of citizens that Jules' acolytes loomed over as they forced them to their knees, their hands bound and heads bowed at the bottom of the stairs that led to the palace. One or two. That was all she had ever dared imagined would betray her, not the *crowd* that had been brought before her. She didn't even dare count how many there were, the fire growing in her heart, fighting against the cold dread that had already taken hold there as her rage threatened to consume her. They would see her fury; they would face her anger at their betrayal. They had hurt her, after all that she had done for them, and now, they would suffer the consequences.

The buzzing—like a million angry bees swarming to protect their nest from an enemy—drew to a crescendo, and Natalia's patience was replaced with her hatred for those who dared to compare *these* ugly things to *her*. The acolytes and priestesses that followed behind her gasped, and she heard them shuffle backwards, putting distance between themselves and Natalia. Her displeasure was palpable, a miasma in the air that all her city would soon be able to taste and feel pulsating through their veins.

She had lost a lot of her power in her fall, but not all. God had underestimated her abilities. He should have *killed* her. He would have been better off that way, rather than leaving His daughter to grow stronger and hate Him more.

Jules and Helena gasped, dropping to their knees as Natalia clenched her fists together, stomped her feet, and screamed. The sound was shrill, piercing. A pulse of pure energy radiated from Natalia's body, causing the sacrilegious pile to fall apart, an avalanche of blasphemy that would soon be purged from existence.

The citizens gathered to witness retribution pressed their hands to their ears against her screams, though even they would not be spared from it. Natalia could see the blood pouring from beneath their hands—their protection futile against the power of her voice—as their ears were assaulted by her tone.

Those who had been bound screamed alongside her as they were forced to take the brunt of her voice and all the power that laid behind it. Their ears bled, their veins bulged as the notes quivered through their bodies, threatening to burst them from within.

No. They would burn; they would *burn* for what they had done, just as she burned with their betrayal. They would know her pain, and they would know what they had done to her. With a flick of her hand, Natalia set the mountain of betrayal on fire, the flames flickering and cracking behind her back as she descended the stairs.

"You ungrateful swine! I shall make you suffer for this; you'll all wish you had remembered your place! I am the most beautiful, the most glorious, the most *powerful* being in existence! I am more than any of you could ever comprehend. What more could you have needed in your lives other than me?!" she shrieked.

With a stomp of her foot, Natalia connected her mind with that of the prisoners at her feet. She found her way deep into their psyche, and settled her magnificent presence deep in the recesses of their memories. She would take everything from them; everything that had ever been good would be wiped away, and they would be left writhing in pain... in the darkness that they had created for themselves.

She stood back, the deed done, the seed of her inner flames planted in the back of their minds. It would eat away at every happy memory they had ever had, leaving them with only their despair and misery as it infected their veins and burned through their very being.

For her victims, it would feel like an eternity, as though time had stopped, while in reality, they would be dead in a matter of minutes. The first horde of traitors threw back their heads and began to scream, writhing against their bonds as the flames ate at their insides. Natalia smiled, casting a glance at the rest of her citizens as they watched in horror at what was happening to those who had dared to defy their goddess.

Natalia snorted and turned away from them; they didn't deserve to look upon her, and she wouldn't even give them that satisfaction in their deaths. They had lost that gift when they turned their backs on her; now, she would turn hers on them.

It took Natalia most of the day to calm the fury raging in her heart. Even after the last screams had died in the air, she trembled in her anger, unable to contain how she felt. Her sisters pressed against their bond to one another, desperate to be let in so that they could speak with her. To taunt her and brag, of that she was certain, but she had no time for them and had no intention of giving them that satisfaction, either. They could wait; she had enough going on without having to deal with *them* as well.

She lied back upon her bed, naked so that she could feel the silk sheets against her skin, cool and soothing compared to the heat of her anger that continued to smoulder in her veins. Natalia raised her hands to her head, her fingertips massaging her temples as she kept her eyes closed.

Beyond the doors, she could hear the whispers of the acolytes and the priestesses, all of them debating whether or not to knock on their Mistress' door and speak with her. She could *feel* their fear even at this distance. That prickling upon her skin as though someone was poking at her with hundreds of tiny needles. She could taste their nervousness in the air, the salt of their sweat tainting her tongue.

Part of her wanted to scare them. Launch herself across the room, throw open the door, and scream at them to go away. To see their faces as all the color drained away, as they cowered from her wrath, whimpering like the pathetic creatures they were.

Yet, there was a part of Natalia that also wanted to coax them into her bedroom, to have her loyal subjects lavish her with their attention. So that they might wash away the stain of the betrayal that she had suffered.

"Do you truly believe you've gotten rid of the problem?" Azazel's smug tone crept into Natalia's head.

Natalia sighed, and she rolled her eyes as she sat up, her hair shivering over her exposed breasts. She'd clearly let her walls slip while she had been trying to calm herself. Keeping her sisters out while controlling her own emotions obviously hadn't been an option, though she'd hoped that neither of her siblings would notice the weakening in her defenses.

"I'm not going to be naïve enough to make that mistake again, Sister. However, I am confident that I have made my point to them," Natalia replied curtly.

"So, you took my advice then? You chose fear over that ridiculous notion of love?"

"No, I chose to make an example of those who had betrayed me, so that the others could remember all the things that I have given them. I gave them eternal life, a gift that all humans have been seeking for… how many millennia since we were tasked to watch over them?"

"Countless, but you gave it to them too freely, Sister. You should have offered it to them as a reward."

"Reward? I wasn't aware you knew of such a word." Natalia snorted. "The great Azazel, Queen of Darkness, when was the last time you rewarded anybody anything? I chose my people for their beauty because they were the worthiest to be in my presence, and I gifted them immortality, so that they might forever be with me. They only ever needed me."

"Worked out well so far. And I reward my civilians. The ones who win my tournaments are allowed to live." Azazel chortled.

Natalia rolled her eyes at her sister's response. Azazel had always enjoyed watching the suffering of others, far more than she should. Her twisted sense of self had left her a manipulative nightmare, finding ways to twist a situation for her own benefit and entertainment. Unlike Raziel and Natalia, Azazel readily let her people cavort with one another, a *reward*, Natalia supposed, was what her sister would class it as. Azazel didn't seek love like Raziel, nor did she expect to be worshipped as Natalia did. All she wanted was to win.

"So, what now, Sister? You've made your point to them. Do you believe you will not lose control again?"

"I never lost it, Azazel. I merely forgot how fickle humans could be. How much attention they required. They never stopped loving me; they just sought other avenues to fill the void left by my magnificence when I cut short my time with them. It was not a loss of control; I do not lose control."

"Ah, yes, the magnificent Natalia never loses control. Does she?"

Natalia could almost hear her sister rolling her eyes across their link, and rolled hers in return.

"No, she doesn't. Anyway, where's Raziel? I'm surprised she hasn't butted in with her opinion, as usual." She snorted, crossing her arms over her naked chest, trying hard not to scowl.

"I have not heard from her. I felt her a few times in the last day or so, but I have not had any contact with her. She's probably found another victim as her latest love ploy and is focusing on that rather than poking fun of you."

Again, Natalia rolled her eyes at her sister's smug tone. She was such an annoyance; she always had been, but Natalia wasn't going to give Azazel the satisfaction of a response. Not this time.

"I'm sure she will come crawling back when she kills them, like she always does. Any of your lot get close to ridding us of your presence yet?"

"Don't be stupid, Sister. As if they could even get close to me. I'm not you."

"No, you're not, nor will you ever be as good as I am," Natalia replied with a smile, flicking her hair over her shoulder. "You've been lucky so far, Azazel. That's all it is, but you'll never be able to beat me. I told you before, I know I'm the best of us. God knew it. That's why He cast me out. He only cast you out because you were a reject and a degenerate. I was a threat to His glory."

"Delusional, as always. Believe what you like, Sister. Raziel and I see you for what you truly are."

"Yes, you better!" Natalia snapped, slamming the walls down on their connection once more, cutting her sister from her mind before Azazel could say another word.

Natalia sighed; she should have known better. The *second* she'd heard Azazel's voice, she should have disengaged. Her sister knew how to rile her; *both* of her sisters did, and Natalia knew she shouldn't give them the time of day. It was only out of common courtesy that she even bothered speaking with them; they were naturally jealous of how wonderful she was, and it was the least she could do to allow them a glimpse of what they could never be.

Strive as they might, they would never surpass her, but at least they would have a common goal. They might better themselves if they tried to emulate her greatness. Such a shame for them that they would never come close to being perfect.

She did wonder about Raziel, however. It was unlike her sister to pass up a chance to join Azazel in trying to get a rise out of Natalia. It wasn't worry that she felt; she didn't worry for her sister—the other fallen angel was as beneath her as everyone else, after all. It was merely because of curiosity. Raziel had *never* let Natalia bring down her walls without poking her oar in alongside Azazel, so for her second sister to remain silent as she had was… odd.

She reached over for her robe, throwing it over her shoulders as she swung her legs off the bed, striding out onto her balcony. Smoke still floated lazily into the sky from the smouldering pile of items that Natalia had burnt earlier in the day.

The flickering sparks that lingered on the burning pages and artwork looked like a swarm of fireflies in the darkness from where Natalia stood. The bodies of the men and women she had destroyed had been removed from the palace steps long before Natalia graced the city with her presence upon the balcony—Jules clearly ordered his acolytes to remove them so that Natalia did not have to look upon them. Good, they weren't worthy of her gaze, let alone another second of her thoughts.

Leaning upon the marble railing of her balcony, Natalia felt the breeze ruffle her curls as she closed her eyes, enjoying the quiet that had returned to her world. Knowing that she was supreme in everything that she ever did.

The city fell unusually quiet over the next couple of days, though Natalia chose to take this as a sign of her rebellious citizens keeping their heads down as they thought about what they had done. They would be in mourning! They had broken her heart, after all, by making these false images that couldn't remotely be compared with her own flawless vision. No, the quiet was nothing to worry about. It was her people showing her their love by not causing any more of a fuss for her, by proving that they were sorry for letting their minds stray from her perfection.

They would work harder to prove their devotion to her from now on, she was sure of that. In fact, she was quite convinced that they were all creating the most beautiful gifts for her in confirmation of their utter love and admiration for her... and her alone.

Natalia remained in her palace, allowing only the acolytes and her priestesses to tend to her. They had never strayed from her side, even after she caused them harm in her anger, and they still wanted to show her how much they adored her. She had been right in letting them care for her all this time, and they would be rewarded with her presence because of their devotion.

Oh, they feared her a little more now, and rightly so, given the show of power that she had displayed for the entire city. She had been gentle with them, reminding them that her wrath had been reserved for those who dared to vilify her city with images of less perfect things than herself.

In the back of her mind, Natalia reminded herself that she would need to grace her people with her presence again, but for now, her absence was their punishment. Maybe this way, they would learn to appreciate the gift that was her existence amongst them. Did they not understand how truly insignificant they were as a race? Had *God* ever graced them with *His* presence personally? No! He hadn't, and He didn't compare to even an ounce of her perfection. He might have been her father, but He was as unworthy of being in her company as these humans were. The difference was that *she* knew they deserved a generous leader—a goddess, in fact—to rule over them and give them something to strive for!

"Oh, Wondrous Vision of Utter Sublimity, might I beg for a moment of your time?" Jules asked.

Natalia smiled, turning to face her Head Priest as he proffered himself at her feet, his fingertips trembling against her toes as he dared to touch her feet in reverence. No matter the display of power she had given, Jules was the same as he had always been with her, and Natalia appreciated that a little more now than she had before.

"What can I do for you, Jules?" she asked, leaning over him with a smile.

A thought crossed her mind that, one of these days, she was going to make him look her in the eyes and see what reaction she could elicit from the man. Natalia imagined his head physically exploding, or Jules wetting himself in his excitement. Would he be premature, given the stimulation of being allowed that close to her? Or would he find a way to perform? Maybe she *would* take up the opportunity to gift Jules a night with her—she would see.

"I do not mean to intrude or to criticize, but I was curious…" He hesitated, and his fingers grew still on her feet. Natalia could tell that he was second-guessing asking her whatever was on his mind.

"It's alright, Jules, go on," she coaxed.

"You said it yourself that it was your lack of presence that caused your people to stray. Is it wise to hide away from them again? Not that you're hiding, or that I am questioning your actions! My Lady obviously knows better than I!" he squealed, suddenly realizing the weight of his words.

Natalia grunted with amusement, though she found herself unable to keep her body from stiffening instinctively. He could say he wasn't questioning her; he could say that he didn't mean the words he'd spoken, but they both knew that wasn't entirely true. Had her lapse in judgment brought doubt into the minds of even her most trusted subjects? No. They *knew* better.

"Of course, I know better than you, Jules; that goes without saying," Natalia replied, though the bitterness at the edge of her words could not be missed despite how softly she spoke to her priest. "This is their punishment, which should go without saying, but I will say it out loud so that you never make the mistake of questioning me again. Yes, my absence may have created this situation, but they know what fate awaits them now if they show the same betrayal as the others did. They will *learn* from that, and in the meantime, they will sit quietly and reflect on what has happened recently. They will remember how *lucky* they are that I deemed them worthy enough to be chosen to live in *my* world. I could have left them to the mercy of my sisters, to a life of never knowing if they were going to see the next day, but I didn't. *I* was merciful. *I* was kind. *I* chose to bring you all into my world and allow you to be in my presence!" Natalia hissed, kicking Jules away from her. "They are going to remember that, and they are going to be grateful. They are going to be *loyal*. They are going to *love* me!"

Jules whimpered from the crumpled heap of fabric he now resembled, cowering against the wall where Natalia had discarded him. His wide eyes stared at her from beneath the hood of his robe, and Natalia recognized the fear that the acolytes and priestesses looked at her with now.

Jules had only ever looked at her in admiration, never in fear. As if he realized that she had noticed, he quickly looked at the floor, his gaze fixed on her reflection rather than her person as he scurried back across the corridor to her. He hurriedly covered her toes and feet in gentle kisses, his fingers caressing her ankles as he continued to whimper and shower her with affection.

"My Lady, forgive me! I meant no offense! I should never have said anything. I did not mean for it to sound as though I did not trust your judgment. You—who is the wisest of all beings in existence, the epitome of perfection—are the one true goddess of all!" He blubbered.

Natalia smiled, cocking her head to one side as she looked down at the pathetic waste of flesh at her feet. She only tolerated their existence in her company because she deserved to be worshipped.

"Remember that, Jules," Natalia whispered, kneeling beside the man, her fingertips brushing against his chin as she forced him to look up at her. "Now, I will let them miss me for a little longer, and then I shall grace my citizens with my beauty so that they might shower me with their love and devotion as I truly deserve. Until then, they can suffer in my absence; that way, they might learn a little humility in the presence of one who surpasses them in every way imaginable."

"You are right as ever, Sublime Beauty of Grandeur. I lost my head for a moment; I beg for your forgiveness."

"Only this once, Jules, but I will not be so kind if you stray from your path again," she hissed, flicking his face away as she stood up and strode down the corridor toward her vault, leaving him to proclaim his adoration of her to all in the palace, at the top of his lungs.

Adorned in the finest silks of deepest red, embellished with gold, Natalia looked exquisite as she strode through her palace. Her reflection smiled at her as she made her way to the entrance, catching flashes of her bare legs as she moved gracefully through the corridors.

Red and gold really *did* suit her; why had she never realized that before? It was such a delicious shade for her, and complimented her ivory skin. Her citizens were going to be in awe of her in this dress!

Smiling, Natalia pushed open the palace doors and hurried out into the dazzling sunshine. It was always sunny in her world, but of course it was, as if *she* would allow something as dark and miserable as rain into her domain. Admittedly, she would still be a shining beacon, regardless of the color of the sky, but she hated rain and dark clouds; it dulled the way her hair shone.

The breeze was gentle and warm as it brushed against her skin, tugging at the loose curls that framed her perfectly sculpted face. She could enjoy the sun and the breeze from her balcony, of course, but it wasn't quite the same as being out in the open, enjoying the sun that reflected off every surface of her dazzling golden city.

Natalia hurried down the steps of the palace, relishing in the warmth of the golden cobbles under her bare feet. It was time to allow her people to see her again, so that they could go back to worshipping her, as was only right.

She made her way through the streets, her hands clasped behind her back, enjoying her own company as her image flickered beside her on every surface. The city was her pride and joy, a perfect example of what she was capable of, and so fitting—considering that it allowed her to be forever surrounded by herself. There was nothing more perfect than she, and that was a fact.

When she came to the square where she had found the first image that was not her own, Natalia stopped and scowled, her brow furrowed as she realized that she hadn't seen a single citizen during her entire time walking through the city. They should have been flooding the streets, eager to be in her company once more! Yet, she had not seen a soul this entire time.

"Where are they all?" Natalia muttered under her breath to her reflections as she turned on the spot, glancing at her statue in the center of the square. "Why are they not out here to greet me?!"

Were they all still afraid? Was that what this was? *Fear.* She had forgiven them! Did they not see this? If she hadn't, she wouldn't have come into the city to allow them the chance to bask in all her wonder!

No. There was something more to this. Had she been wrong? Had she *still* read this situation wrong? Samuel had warned her—hadn't he? That this was so much deeper than just missing her, but she had chosen to ignore his words for her own answers because only she could be right. Yet the emptiness of the city, the lack of people crowding to be around her, told Natalia otherwise.

Something was not right in her world, and the doubt was finding its way back into her heart.

Natalia had never felt so exposed in her life. Standing in the square, with no one in sight, she felt as though a thousand eyes were trained solely upon her.

"You, self-conscious? I never thought I'd live to see the day!" Azazel's pompous tone slithered its way into Natalia's mind.

She took a step toward the fountain in the center of the square. Restored to its former glory—just as the building she had smashed a hole through had been—her reflection staring back at her, wide-eyed and… fearful? No! She didn't feel fear; what did she have to be afraid of?! *She* was in charge here, *she* was the leader of this world, and *she* was the one in charge. All eyes *should* be on her, so that they could bask in the glory of her magnificence!

So, why did it feel so… wrong?

"This has really shaken you, Sister. Normally, I would take such great pleasure in all of this… but I have never seen you like this. It's… disturbing."

"Not half as disturbing for you as it is for me." Natalia growled under her breath, throwing up her defensive walls to keep her sisters out while she composed herself.

She was used to Azazel's ribbing, but even that had felt stunted compared to what she usually expected from her sibling. It wasn't like Azazel to hold *back* in her prodding, not since the three of them had fallen and chosen to make their own worlds.

They had been at odds ever since, trying to outdo one another and prove that they were the superior sister. Natalia knew she was better than they were, and she felt the need to let Azazel and Raziel strive to prove their points, futile as they were.

Yet, Natalia had felt her sister bite her tongue, as though she had chosen *not* to go down her usual route of winding Natalia up. It wasn't normal; in fact, it was almost as unnerving as the silence that filled her city.

And where was Raziel?! Never, in all of their years since their separation, had *one* sister taken the time to wind the other up without the third sticking their nose in as well. Twice now, Natalia had spoken with Azazel without Raziel's presence. It was unnatural; it was wrong!

"Everything is wrong." Natalia scowled, striding out of the square as she walked purposefully down another street, wondering if she might find her citizens elsewhere.

Natalia could feel her anger swelling inside herself at the continued lack of presence from her people. They should have been throwing themselves at her *feet* and proclaiming their love for her, and yet, there hadn't even been a *whisper* of their existence. She knew they were there. It wasn't as if they had anywhere else to go; her city was the only place in the world, and it *was* the world.

Every street, every square, every alleyway she walked down, was empty of everything but her own reflection. Never, in all of her existence, had Natalia loathed seeing herself more than she did now. She looked divine, and there was no one to gasp and coo and aww at her as there should have been. She knew she was scowling; she could feel a knot forming between her eyes, and she couldn't bear to look at herself. Her angry face was not attractive, and the lines that would form would only fuel her rage further.

"Fine. Be childish, all of you. I'll leave you all to wallow in your misery, and then we'll see how well you all do, hm?" Natalia huffed, flicking her dark curls over her shoulder with her hand as she turned toward her palace. "You'll regret this," she hissed.

A smile flickered across her features, and Natalia giggled darkly as she stared at her grinning reflection. There was mischief in those sapphire eyes of hers, and it was delightful.

"I gave you all a gift because you were the most beautiful humans in existence. You were all as close to perfection as humans could be, though you would never meet *my* standards. No one could! I wonder how well you'll all fare if I take away your looks and my gifts, and leave you all to rot in despair. Maybe then, you'll learn your place in this world. You'll all come crawling back to me, begging for my forgiveness, but I wonder if I'll feel as inclined to grant it." She snorted.

Oh, how wicked she could be, but they had to learn the way of the world, and they seemed to have forgotten it. She would make them remember how *good* they had it because of her.

Natalia watched her reflection as she lifted her hand, wiggling her fingers as though waving at the woman staring back at her. She was already the most beautiful creature in existence. Well, now, she was going to ensure that *everyone* remembered that.

Inhaling deeply, Natalia closed her eyes and focused on her inner calm, quashing the tidal wave of emotions that threatened to overwhelm her. She was in control, she was the master of this place, and she was going to prove it to everyone, just as she had a thousand times before. She had let her sisters plant their seeds of doubt, but no longer. Natalia was in charge here.

Her breathing slowed as she reached deep into herself, focusing on drawing her powers out. It wasn't as easy as it had been when she was in Heaven, but no matter. As far as Natalia was concerned, her ability to still utilize her powers —despite her father's attempt to hobble her—only proved her point that *she* was the most powerful being in existence. She was better than He was. He may have clipped her wings, but He hadn't stifled her brilliance—merely hindered it slightly.

Natalia felt the swell of her power deep in her stomach and rising to her chest, and she smiled. She spread her arms wide, her palms toward the sky. As the surge within reached its apex, Natalia slammed her hands together with a thunder-like crack that echoed throughout the entire city, the ground shuddering against the force of her powers. She heard the city gasp in shock as the ground trembled at her magnificence, followed by the collective screams of her citizens as the realization of what she had done became apparent to them. They would never forget their place again, not after this.

Opening her eyes, Natalia winked at the wickedly smiling image of herself as she strode toward her palace with a satisfied look upon her smug face. They would come crawling back soon enough, and when they did, she would consider whether or not to forgive them for their betrayals. For now, she would enjoy their screams, for it was music to her ears.

"M-my Lady?" Jules stammered as he greeted Natalia atop the steps of the palace, though his attention appeared to be fixated on the screaming city beyond.

Natalia grinned as she looked at her Head Priest, his hood pulled back from his ashen face, his eyes wide and filled with fear. The residents of her palace were left immune to her little punishment; the priests and priestesses had remained loyal. Jules may have made the mistake of questioning her when he shouldn't have, but his devotion to her was unwavering, and she would reward him for *that*, at least.

She came to stand beside him, draping one arm over his

shoulders, the other hand resting gently on the shoulder closest to her as she pressed her body against his arm. Her eyes followed his gaze as the city continued to scream, the level of hysteria rising amongst the rest of her citizens. Their fear was almost palpable. Natalia could have sworn she tasted the metallic tinge of sweat and dismay from where she stood.

"Wh-what's happened, Magnificent One?" Jules stammered.

She watched her priest out of the corner of her eye, amused as she spotted his glance toward her and away again. Now *his* fear, she *could* taste. He could act as strong as he liked, but there was no hiding his true feelings from her, not when she could feel his body quivering under her half-embrace. Good. She hadn't punished Jules, nor the acolytes, but they would all cement their place in their minds, given the punishment that the rest of the city was now enduring.

"I walked amongst them, as I promised I would, and not one of them came out to honor me as I expected. I will not be disrespected, Jules, not by anyone. Least of all, the insects I have taken pity on, and given such lavish gifts to as I have all these years. So, they are learning a lesson, one I hope I will never have to repeat since it is so ugly in nature, but one that they clearly all require." She sighed, resting her head on her hand and looking up at the priest through her lashes.

"A lesson?" he asked, glancing down at her.

Natalia giggled. She stood upright, planting a kiss on Jules' cheek. The priest whimpered, his knees giving way beneath him as he pressed his lips to Natalia's bare feet over and over and over again in thanks for her affection and attention.

"Yes, a lesson. Find Helena. I want you both to take your acolytes and priestesses into the city to witness the punishment that I have spared you all from. See with your own eyes the fate that shall await anyone who dare to defy me further. My patience has run out, order will be restored, and they will remember who their goddess is." Natalia smiled, gently removing her foot from Jules' desperate advances, striding back into the embrace of the palace. "Go now, Jules, and remind my people who is in charge here. Show them what loyalty and love can reward, as you and the rest of the palace have been left immune. Tell them that it's time they remember who they are loyal to, and that such indiscretions will not be ignored again."

"Y-yes, my Lady. I shall fetch them now," Jules replied.

He scurried past her, his head kept low, back bent in respect as he hurried into the palace to do as she had requested. She would leave him to see the fruits of her labor with his own eyes; it would have more impact if they saw it themselves, rather than Natalia describing what she had done.

It was a good day to be a god.

The haggard expressions on the faces of Natalia's loyalists told her everything she needed to know about how they felt in terms of the punishment that she'd dished out to the rest of the city. Together, the acolytes and priestesses shuffled back through the Throne Room, bowing instinctively to their Mistress, though Natalia felt it was a little shallow.

She wasn't angry at them; however, she'd expected them to be a bit deflated on their return. The reality of what she had done to the rest of the world had been shoved in their faces, the terror and hysteria of the city within their reach. They were safe, but only as long as they loved her, and how could they not love her after everything she did for them all?

It was alright. They'd learn now.

Jules and Helena walked in, arm-in-arm, clearly using the other to stay upright. It was somewhat surprising to see the pair so close, considering their silent rivalry for Natalia's affection, but it convinced Natalia that her punishment was just. If these two could get over their usual squabbles and help one another through the shock, then the rest of her citizens would realize the severity of their actions and come crawling back to her for forgiveness. It wouldn't be long before they were showering her with their undying love and affection once again.

"Well?" Natalia asked, inspecting her pristine fingernails in a nonchalant fashion, her legs hanging over one arm of her throne as she sat casually upon it.

"The city is in turmoil, my Lady. The people are...," Helena began, her hand over her heart as though that would stop it from racing.

Natalia grinned as she swung her legs around, facing her Head Priest and Priestess properly, her fingers laced together on her lap.

"They're what, Helena?" Natalia asked in a jovial tone.

The pair flinched, clearly taken aback by how happy she seemed, but why wouldn't she be? Had she not rectified her mistake? She had allowed complacency, and now she had fixed it. They would never, *ever*, forget who their loyalty and love should be reserved for. Not anymore.

"They're *ugly*," Helena scoffed, her nose wrinkling in disdain.

"They're old," Jules added quietly, his body shuddering visibly at the thought.

"They're how they would be if it wasn't thanks to *me*." Natalia sighed, pushing herself off the throne and spinning around with a gleeful giggle. "I gave them life, *eternal* life, and I kept them fit and healthy, and all I ever asked for was that they love me in return. I gave them perfection and allowed them a taste of what they *could* be, and all I wanted was for them to admire my splendor as I was due. It wasn't a lot to ask for; how could they not adore me? *Look* at me! And yet, even after I punished the others and deprived them of my presence, they turned their backs on me when I gave them time to be beside me." Natalia tutted and shook her head, glancing back at Jules and Helena over her shoulder with a grin. "They won't forget now. They will see how ugly their actions have been, and they will ache and weep for the beauty that they had taken from them. And once they've learnt their place, I'll think about returning their lives to them as they were."

"M-my Lady...," Helena began, her words halting before they started.

In the reflection of the walls and floor, Natalia spotted the glance between Helena and Jules, and she raised an eyebrow at it. Never in all their years together had Helena looked to *Jules* before speaking to Natalia.

"Speak!" Natalia snapped, turning on the pair like a viper in the sand snatching its prey.

"I worry that many will take their lives. Seeing them with our own eyes... the heartache that they are clearly suffering, the despair," Helena whispered.

"Then let them. Only those *worthy* of being in my presence will remain. Let those grotesque people die if that's what they wish to do; it will only prove that they were not meant to bask in my magnificence!" Natalia snorted. "If they had ever been truly beautiful, they would know better. Anyway, I have spent my day in the vaults, now I want a bath. Tend to me, Helena. And Jules? I will see you in my chamber tonight," Natalia cooed, giggling as the Head Priest's eyes widened, threatening to pop straight out of their sockets with the shock.

Loyalty would be rewarded, and tonight, he would finally have his prize.

The door to her chamber opened, and Natalia giggled as she shifted on her bed, swinging around onto her stomach to face the door as Jules shuffled nervously inside. He closed the door behind him and remained there for a moment, his back pressed against the ornate entryway, his face hidden beneath his hood.

It amused Natalia to see him so apprehensive. He never had the confidence that Helena did in her presence, but he was more nervous than usual. As he remained unmoved, Natalia rolled her eyes and laughed aloud, the sound pleasant as it echoed back at her in the enormous room. She crawled to the edge of the bed, slowly, grinning as she spotted him glance up at her and look away again when he saw her naked frame. He'd seen her this way a thousand times before, but this was the only time she had sought to seduce *him*.

"Come now, Jules, we've waited a long time for this day. Won't you look at me?" She purred at him as she slid off the bed and began to saunter across the room toward her Head Priest. "I know you've been waiting for tonight, so why are you so hesitant?"

"I… I have imagined this for so long, my Lady. I just never believed that it would come true," Jules whimpered, wringing his hands as he kept glancing up from the floor to Natalia and back down again, not quite able to meet her eyes.

"Oh, Jules, good things always come to those who wait," Natalia continued huskily as she reached for him, sliding her hands up his chest, slightly irked by the robe he wore that remained between them. "And I'm the best thing of all; I'm *always* worth the wait," she whispered, her hands reaching up to remove the hood from the man's handsome face.

"You won't be worth a *damn* thing soon enough!" A voice shouted from behind.

Natalia hissed, relinquishing her grip of Jules as she spun around to face the intruder. How did they even get into her private bed chamber?! Had they been hiding this entire time? Just waiting for her and Jules to be alone?!

The sight that met Natalia was utterly repulsive, and she gave a small shriek of horror at the shriveled man before her. Hunch backed, his skin laid loosely on his bony frame, his withered body covered in deep wrinkles that left his eyes looking sunken into his skull. She had stripped her citizens of their natural born beauty, leaving them withering and old, on the brink of death with every breath they took. She'd known they would be disgusting, but actually seeing one of them with her own eyes was another thing entirely!

"How did you get in here?!" She snarled, nose wrinkled in

disgust as she stepped back against Jules, wanting to put as much distance between her and the shrunken man before her as possible.

"By sheer force of will and determination. Not just mine, but the city's as well. We've had enough of you; it's time you paid for *your* sins." The man snapped in return, raising a shaky hand above his head with a dark smile upon his leathery face, a glass bottle glistening in his hand. "The time has come, the time we've all been waiting for, the time of liberation!" he shouted.

Natalia gasped as Jules roughly grasped her by the shoulders, his fingernails digging into her delicate skin as he all but tossed her aside. She grunted as she fell indignantly to the ground, skidding along the polished golden floor a few feet from where she had been standing. Her head whipped around, ready to admonish Jules for such blasphemy.

But any thoughts of reprimand that she may have had vanished as her Head Priest screamed loudly, his body quivering as he writhed against the door, clawing at the robe that covered his body.

It took the fallen archangel a moment to realize what was happening, but when the realization hit her, she screamed. Whatever the citizen had been holding, had been thrown at Jules—though it had been meant for her. If it hadn't been for the priest's quick thinking, she would have been the victim of the contents of the bottle instead… and that would have been a fate worse than death for Natalia.

She scurried backwards as Jules swung in her direction. If she had thought their assailant was horrific, it was nothing in comparison to the sight that stood before her now. The hood had fallen back from Jules' face, or what was left of it. Huge chunks of flesh had been eaten away by the oozing green liquid that dripped onto the floor, along with blood and bits of the Head Priest's cheek. His lips were completely gone, leaving a perpetual, *terrible* smile on the poor man's face. His eyes, barely held in his skull now that his eyelids had melted, stared at Natalia in horror and desperation, one hand reaching out to her for aid while the other clawed at what remained of his face.

"Stay away! Get away from me!" Natalia howled, physically repulsed by the man's appearance as she scurried to her feet and hurried to the safety of her bed.

"That should have been *you*!" the assailant hissed, reaching behind his back to produce a dagger. "To make you as ugly on the outside as you are on the *inside*."

That word.

That *one* word.

That was all it took for Natalia to snap out of herself and return to her composure. She turned her stunning gaze on the wilted man, her lip curling with her loathing. Out of the corner of her eye, Natalia saw Jules collapse forward onto his face. A crumpled, bloodied mess of the man he'd once been. This *creature* had robbed her of her evening *and* of her Head Priest, and she couldn't allow that, let alone the slight upon her! She would *never* be ugly; she was *perfect*.

Natalia strode across the room toward the man, too quick for him to react beyond gasping as her hand shot out to grip his throat tightly, her nails digging into his sagging flesh. She drew him closer to her, despite her revulsion at his very existence, as she glared down at him.

"I'll show you what ugly really looks like." She snarled.

As her door flew open—clearly by the arrival of the acolytes and priestesses who had been banished from the vicinity to allow Natalia and Jules their time alone—Natalia launched the offender straight out of her bedroom window. His frail body soared through the air and straight into the open world beyond her balcony, his screams fading as he fell onto the street below. There was a soft, yet sickening, crunch as he met his end, but that was drowned out by Natalia's infuriated roar.

On the horizon beyond her palace, the city was ablaze, glowing golden as smoke rose toward the sky. Her punishment hadn't been enough, and now her people were rebelling. She could feel, deep in her heart, that her powers were waning and that she was losing control of them. What more could she do?

Natalia hugged her knees to her chest as she watched Helena direct Jules' acolytes to remove the disturbing remains of their Head Priest from her chamber. She could not bring herself to watch as they turned him over, not wanting to sully her vision or her memory further than it already had been.

There were several gasps when they turned over Jules' body to reveal the extent of the attack, and several of the acolytes wretched and vomited. If that was their reaction, Natalia had no need to look for herself.

She rested her head on her knee, scowling as she half-listened to Helena's instructions to the others, and whispered words about acid of some kind or other. It didn't matter *what* had done that to Jules; the only thing that mattered to Natalia was that it had been meant for *her,* and that she'd been robbed of one of her most devoted subjects. How *dare* these rebels steal Jules from her like this?! He had known how to show true reverence to her magnificence, and now he was gone. Helena would do what she could, but she had never been quite as eloquent with her names for Natalia as Jules had been.

"Barricade the doors and windows! I don't want anyone else getting into the palace unless I, or our Lady, says otherwise!" Helena snapped, causing Natalia to sniffle.

The man had made some sort of grappling hook, shimmying his way up the rope with what little strength he must have had left, in order to get onto her balcony. Natalia had never once closed the window to her bedroom, preferring to feel the fresh air that blew through it—feeling as close to the freedom of flying as she could that way. They had robbed her of *that* as well.

The smoke still rose outside of the palace proper, and the screams and shouts of the rebellious factions defiled Natalia's ears. There were still a few loyal citizens, beyond those who remained in the palace, clearly having learnt from their punishment. Losing their immortality and having their looks stripped away had obviously reminded them that Natalia was their one true love, and now they screamed and begged at her door for aid.

Yet none of them had come to see her when she visited the city streets. Had they *just* bowed down and worshipped her like they were supposed to, none of this would be happening!

A few of the priestesses asked Helena whether they should let those seeking help into the palace, but one dark look from Natalia had said it all. No one was going to be allowed in, not now; no one outside of the palace walls could be trusted. How could they tell if there wasn't a spy amongst them? Someone looking to get inside to harm Natalia, just as that man had?

"My Lady, should I draw you a bath?" Helena asked.

"No. Just go away." Natalia snarled, not wanting to look at the woman.

"But my Lady, we need to make sure that none of the acid touched your precious skin."

"GO AWAY!" Natalia roared, the palace shaking with her ferocity as she turned on her priestess.

"As you wish…," Helena whimpered, bowing her head and scurrying out of the room after the others, closing the door behind her.

Natalia began to scream, thumping her soft bedspread with her fists and kicking her feet just like any toddler having a tantrum would. This wasn't supposed to happen to her! She was perfection, she was splendor, and she was *amazing*! Why could these fools not just recognize that?!

"You are not alone, Sister."

"Raziel?! Where have you been?" Natalia replied, stopping short in her shrieking, eyes wide in shock at her sister's sudden intrusion. "I've had to put up with Azazel's nonsense, but you were not there; it's so unlike you."

"I had my own things to deal with; it's not always about you," Raziel replied.

It had always amazed Natalia how her sister could sound emotionless, yet angry, at the same time. There was always a subtle change in the intonation of her sister's monotone that Natalia had managed to pick up over the centuries. It was minute, barely noticeable, but of course, Natalia had spotted it where others wouldn't.

"Must have been dire if the ever-impulsive Raziel was unable to come and spit her barbs at us. If that had been me,

I'd have made the time; can't have you two thinking you've bested me." Azazel's smug tone snorted.

"Yes, well, I am not you, Sister. I do not need to prove myself to either of you."

"Enough! Both of you. Something is wrong, and I can't be the only one feeling this way." Natalia sighed.

She didn't like admitting it; she'd been pushing the doubt to the back of her mind—along with that niggling feeling of something else that she didn't want to admit existed.

"No, you are not. Something *is* wrong. Many of my people are now able to pull away from my influence. None of them are meant to be able to form relationships outside of the ones I allow, but that is no longer the case," Raziel replied, her tone almost bored.

"It is the same for me here. I thought the punishment that I had given them would be enough, but one of them attacked me last night and killed my Head Priest by accident."

"What punishment?" Azazel asked, her voice dripping with excitement, as though she might be able to use it herself.

"I stole their beauty from them. Nothing that you would have any use of, I'm sure. I thought they would realize how foolish they had been and beg me to restore what little good looks they once had. They would never match me, but I've made them purposefully ugly, and rather than beg for my forgiveness, they have turned on me. Not all, but most. They've set fire to my city, and they call for my blood. The assailant dared to say that he was going to make me as ugly on the outside as he thinks I am on the inside." Natalia snarled, her lips curling as she remembered the exchange.

"Just you slipping, Sister. Nothing for the rest of us to worry about." Azazel snorted.

"Except it's happening to all of us. There's no use denying it, Azazel. If it's happening to Natalia and I, then it's happening to you also."

Natalia smiled, licking her lips in excitement as Raziel turned on their sibling. It was also so satisfying to have the pair go at one another rather than at her.

"So, what do you propose? Come, Natalia, you're the one who suggested this venture in the first place, the one who wanted to prove her powers to the rest of us. How do you suggest we fix what appears to be broken?" Azazel cooed, clearly feeding Natalia's ego, though Natalia was more than happy to allow her sister to fuel the fire in her heart.

That was the problem, though. It was happening to all of them, and Natalia was unsure of how to fix the issue.

Natalia had cut contact with her sisters abruptly, not willing to let them think that she had completely lost her control—not yet—because she *hadn't*. Not entirely. She could feel the tether to her citizens slipping from her fingers, and now that she thought about it, Natalia realized that even her powers were beginning to wane.

She hadn't wanted to admit how tired she'd been when she had punished the city, and hadn't wanted to concede that it had taken a great deal of effort to gather her powers in order to enact it in the first place. Natalia and her sisters had gathered together to create their three separate worlds to show God that they were better than He was, that He had made a mistake when He'd banished them from Heaven.

Was it merely the length of time since their fall that was causing the blip she now felt? Like a tear had been made in the fabric of her world, and everything she had known for certain was now slipping through the cracks like water through her fingers…

No! No. Not her, this didn't happen to *her*. She was the superior being here. The more she let this doubt creep into her heart, the more it was affecting her; that was all this was… wasn't it?

But it wasn't just happening to her. Raziel had said it herself, that she was struggling to keep control of her own citizens now. Her sister's apathy had infected her people from the very beginning; it was Raziel's way of keeping them under her control while she searched for something more for herself.

Her sister's futile hunt for love and emotions that were not within her capacity had gone on for centuries, long before even their fall from grace. She had been caught by God during her examination of humans and their emotions, hence her banishment. But her own world hadn't yielded any more answers. Was there an inkling of fear finally finding its way into Raziel's heart? Was that why she was starting to lose control?

The three of them had always been so self-assured. Maybe that was what this was. They had all become complacent, and then begun to doubt themselves in their own ways, and because of that, they were unable to focus and keep control.

Yes. That made sense. Natalia had *never* doubted her own brilliance until Samuel and her sisters' interference. This was all *their* doing. No more contact! She was putting an end to their influence in her life once and for all. She *knew* she was better than them; she always had been. There was no need in continuing to prove it to them. Let them live in their delusions that they could ever match up to her glory; they wouldn't even come *close*.

Natalia snorted and flicked her hair over her shoulder, staring at her reflection in the wall and smiling. She was beautiful. She bit her bottom lip as she turned slightly, extending one of her legs so that she could admire its elegance and the curve of her buttocks. Her hands flickered over her flawless, pale skin, and she sighed softly as she took the moment to enjoy the image of herself and how perfect she truly was.

She arched her back and pressed her arms against her breasts to make them push out more, pouting and blowing herself a kiss as she giggled slightly. The last few days had been terrible, but she remained as impeccable as ever, despite the amount of scowling she had done. She'd expected lines to form between her eyes from the constant knot that had settled between her brows, but it appeared that her body was even more immaculate than she had expected, and even the stress couldn't dull her allure.

There, that felt better already! It had been her sisters' nonsense infecting her, that was all, leaving a foul blemish on her heart and stifling her majesty. This was why they had separated the worlds, because together, they would have ruined everything that Natalia knew she could achieve. She didn't need them, and now, they would have to suffer an eternity without her.

Natalia gasped and reached a hand out to the wall beside her as the ground beneath her feet shook violently, a deafening clap of thunder echoing through her bed chamber seconds before the glass shattered in the windows. Thousands of tiny, shimmering shards tinkled onto the floor, biting crystals that threatened to cut her fair skin and leave her feet marred forever should she step on them.

She squealed irritably, stepping back from the dangerous shards as her eyes shot to the now empty window frames... and the rising smoke in the center of the city. No! She was in control; she had *fixed* the issue! They shouldn't still be rioting; they couldn't be, now that she knew why her powers had faltered!

Natalia ran to her balcony, stopping only when the minefield of glass glistened at her in the corner of her eye, daring her to come closer. She couldn't risk it; she would never forgive herself for damaging her precious figure.

Looking around, Natalia found a pair of slippers that had been gifted to her eons ago. She had never worn the things, preferring the freedom of bare feet when she walked, and so she had discarded them to one side of the room by her dresser. They had remained there, forgotten and useless, becoming part of the furnishings in her room. Never would Natalia have ever believed that they would be just what she needed, but in that moment, she was oddly grateful that she hadn't told Helena or Jules to dispose of the footwear.

She hurried to the dresser where they had been placed, slipping her feet into the ornate golden slippers. She blinked in surprise at how comfortable they truly were, then chided herself silently for the distraction, dragging herself back to reality when the ground shook with the force of another explosion.

Natalia was forced to grip her dresser tightly to keep herself from falling over, and she snarled, her lips curling in irritation at this attack. This was a slight against *her*, and she would not tolerate it!

Armed with her new footwear, Natalia hurried over to her balcony, stepping carefully over the broken glass. The last thing she wanted to do was accidentally kick up some of the shards and cut herself, despite her caution. She slid past the hanging frames, their remaining glassy teeth gleaming at her as she made sure not to get too close. Once she was outside, the balcony was blissfully free of anything harmful, and Natalia hurried to the edge. Clinging to the marble railing, she leaned over and stared at the chaos below.

The city was burning, the people were rioting, and her punishment appeared to have been revoked from several of those trying to knock down her main door. Things were worse than she had realized.

atalia made her way back into her chamber, kicking the slippers from her feet once she was back on clear floors. Hurrying to the door, she threw it open so hard that she tore it from its hinges. One collapsed to the ground with an almighty clatter, while the other swung around to lean against the wall.

Whatever, she didn't have time to worry about such things. She needed to speak with Helena; she needed to deal with the insurgents outside her palace.

"Mistress!" a voice called out from behind her, and Natalia wheeled around to face an acolyte. "Mistress, please. Priestess Helena believes that you would be safest in the vault; we can protect you there," the young man whispered, bowing his head as he dropped to his knees at her feet.

"No. If they think they can intimidate me, *me*, then they are sorely mistaken. I am stronger than they are; this entire *city* could not match my strength. I have never needed to use my physical strength before. Well, not until much more recently, but even then, none of you have seen the true extent of what I am capable of. And now, it's time I prove to these fools that I *am* the true god in this world, and if that means physically ripping them limb from limb, then so be it." Natalia snarled, turning away.

"But… but Mistress!" the young man whimpered, but Natalia took no notice as she strode away. "Please, it's for your own safety! None of us wants you to risk yourself with the disloyal. Let *us* deal with them! It's our job, our duty, our *privilege* to take care of you!" he called after her, but she still did not halt in her purpose.

She could hear the pitter-patter of his footfalls as he hurried after her, muttering under his breath as he clearly tried to find the words to reason with her. Reason was gone. Now, she had to use the ugliest of her powers and get physical with these rebels.

Had they forgotten that she was an angel? Fallen or otherwise, she had been created by God, shaped to be the perfect being. God had just gone a little too far with her. He'd outdone himself and given her too much power, hence her exile. Well, she would remind these petty, pathetic humans of this fact. She would beat it into them until they saw that she was the embodiment of perfection in every way.

They. Would. Learn.

Natalia made her way across the Throne Room, her footfalls silent in comparison to the thudding steps of the acolyte. The air was almost electric with his fear; it was so apparent that Natalia felt it tingling against her skin. For a moment, she considered grabbing him by the scruff of his robe and throwing him straight out into the crowd that waited on her doorstep, but she reminded herself that he was merely human. He couldn't comprehend her strength and resolve, and his worry came from a deep-seated love for her. So really, she couldn't blame him for it, let alone snap at him over it. He was one of her truly loyal followers, and since she had lost Jules, she could do with keeping him around.

Odd, how she missed the priest, now that he was gone. She really had grown used to having him at her heels. He hadn't deserved such a terrible fate; he couldn't even make a beautiful corpse now.

"Move the barricade," Natalia commanded, waving her hand at the priestesses and acolytes gathered by the quivering doors.

The array of furniture and golden statues of herself that had been dragged against the door to keep it shut shivered with every attempt the rebels made to bring the doors down. As if Natalia would create an entranceway that could be brought down by the hands of weak men and women? What did they take her for? Snorting, she stood before the mound of items blocking her way, her eyes flickering over her gathered followers, all of whom were staring at her in disbelief.

"Bu-but my Lady!" one of the Priestesses squealed, her hand at her throat as she looked from Natalia to the mound currently keeping the angry mass at bay.

"You heard me," Natalia replied slowly and quietly, menace tainting her usually sweet tone.

There was no time to argue with the fearful. She had something she needed to do, and she was going to get it done.

"Do as your Lady says! How dare you question her

wisdom?!" Helena's sharp tone echoed through the Throne Room.

Natalia smiled, turning her head slightly to glance at her Head Priestess from over her shoulder. There was the Helena she knew well. Bold, beautiful, and full of confidence. It was this surety that made Helena better-looking in Natalia's eyes, as though it caused her to glow.

"My Lady, we will move the barricade enough to open one of the doors, just enough to let you out. It will allow us to keep the disloyal out; we do not wish the palace to be overrun." Helena added with a firm nod.

"Of course. I will not allow this *scum* to sully our halls with their presence, but I will cast them from my door," Natalia purred, taking a deep, satisfying breath as she smiled. "And then we will begin the arduous task of reminding each and every one of them who I am. For too long, I've left them to their own devices, clearly. Well, no longer."

"My Lady?" Helena glanced at Natalia, surprise flickering briefly across her face, along with something that Natalia suspected was fear.

"You will see. But first, I will deal with this mob." Natalia sighed, stepping forward as the acolytes and priestesses made a path to the door, gripping the huge circular handle in readiness.

Natalia gave a nod of her head and waited for them to open the door just enough for her slight figure to slip through without grazing her precious skin. The second the door shifted, the mutinous mass beyond saw their chance and began to press forward, desperate to get through the gap and into the Palace. But Natalia wasn't going to allow that to happen; they weren't going to set one *toe* inside.

Quick as a flash, Natalia made her move. As the first of the anarchists shoved their way through the door, they found themselves wedged between one another and the structure itself, and they were met with the wrath of their goddess. In the back of her mind, Natalia worried about getting physical, ever conscious of damaging her skin or marking it in any fashion. It was why she despised having to use her physical strength.

She'd hated it as an angel, expected to be a soldier whenever God called upon her for such menial tasks. The war with Lucifer had almost destroyed her, not because of the blood and gore she came back to Heaven covered in, but because she constantly had to fight to keep the demons from cutting her skin. Though it had made her a fine soldier, in a way, no one could dodge and parry a blow like Natalia could. Just another feather in the cap of perfection for her. It didn't make her loathe it any less.

She stepped into their field of vision; her dark smile reflected back at her in their wide, terrified eyes. They knew what was coming; how could they not? They had upset her, and she was going to hurt them as much as they had hurt her… and then some.

With the flat of her palm, Natalia slammed her hand into the face of the first man, enjoying the nauseating crunch that his nose made as it shattered from the blow. Blood, hot and sticky, exploded onto her palm as she decimated his nose, leaving only a crater and hanging flesh in the place it had once been. His screams barely registered, nor did the grunt of the man behind him—who found himself headbutted when the first man's head shot backwards at him.

They stumbled back out of the door and onto the open steps. The path was clear, and Natalia slipped through the gap to join the mutinous bunch that waited for her. Some were as wizened as she had expected them to be, as they *all* should have been, yet some seemed to have regained their strength and their good looks. But how? How had her punishment been revoked without *her* saying so?!

Natalia growled and sprang to action, remembering the attack the night before by the man with the bottle, and the state of Jules' face as his flesh and bone were eaten away by the liquid. They would pay for this. They would all pay, and she would take that payment with their lives. The survivors would be the lucky ones; they would learn what a merciful god truly looked like, and they would be given the chance to love her again. They would be devoted; they would be loyal; they would be *hers*.

A blind rage swallowed Natalia as she got her hands dirty, literally. The red mist that blurred her vision was one she hadn't encountered in a *very* long time, and even her sisters hadn't been able to entice it out of her, despite their constant jabbing. The last time she had truly lost her mind to her anger had been just before her fall, when she argued with God and their other siblings, and fought her way out of the Gates of Heaven. God had taken her wings, but *she* had fought for her own freedom and made her way to Earth. He'd been powerless to stop that, and now, *they* would be powerless to stop *her*.

She was a whirlwind of perfect moves. Every time they tried to swarm her, clearly hoping that they would win through sheer numbers alone, she found a way to distance herself from them or push them back. They couldn't get close enough to the tornado that was Natalia to land a blow. A couple of the rebels tried to launch themselves at her from opposite angles, but Natalia caught them and threw them into the wall of their companions, pushing them back from the doors of her palace and sending them stumbling down the steps to the street below.

The crowd stepped back a little, hesitating as they realized that they were out of their league. Natalia watched their resolve waver, but she could see in their eyes that the fires of rebellion still raged on. They weren't ready to give up; this was their chance, and she could see it written on their faces. Did they really think they could win this fight? Why could they not understand how good they all had it under her rule?!

"Ignorant pigs!" She spat at them, the rage swelling in her chest, her heart racing painfully.

"I'd rather be an ignorant pig than beholden to someone as *hideous* as you," a soft, feminine voice whispered from behind her.

Natalia jumped. Her rage had clouded her vision and her ability to think rationally. She had allowed one of them to get behind her, to get *close*. Out of the corner of her eye, Natalia caught a glint of glass, and her heart fell through the floor. She knew what that bottle contained; she had seen what it had done to her beloved Jules.

"No!" another voice screamed.

Before Natalia could react, the acolyte who had begged her to remain safe in the vault threw himself out of the door, slamming his body against the woman.

Natalia whipped around as the pair screamed and writhed at her feet, the terrible contents eating at their flesh the second the bottle had shattered from their fall. Her gaze fixed on that of the acolyte, and she saw the plea in his expression just as she had in Jules, but this time, she knew that even if she got involved, it was too late.

She ripped the offender away from the acolyte, sending her flailing body down the steps and into the crowd, though she did not go as far as Natalia had intended.

Why did she ache so much? Had someone managed to land a blow?! No… it was her strength itself. She was *panting*.

How had she not realized it before? That brief pause had caused the rage to dissipate for a moment, just long enough for the rest of her body to catch up and realize how exhausting this all was. Her heart pounded in her chest, and her lungs burned with every breath, her breathing quick and labored from the sheer effort of fighting off these rebellious citizens of hers.

No. This couldn't be happening, not to her! She had never grown tired in a fight. She had never slowed, not even in the war. They had fought for several months at a time, with no respite, and she had never faltered during that entire time.

Dark tendrils crept into her mind, icy hands gripping her heart as the doubt resurfaced. She was kidding herself if she thought she wasn't losing her power; she could see that now.

Her hesitation was all it took for one of the rebels to launch himself at her, a glistening golden dagger held high above his head. For a moment, the darkness in Natalia's heart threatened to let him kill her. How could she go on living if she wasn't completely perfect? She couldn't live flawed; that wasn't who she was. Just as the tip of the blade plunged toward her chest, the acolyte, halfway to death but still loyal enough to protect his goddess, grabbed the man by the leg and caused him to stumble.

Natalia reacted, her hand snapping up to grab the assailant by the wrist. In one fluid motion, she elbowed the man in the stomach and flung him over her shoulder before scooping up the dying acolyte, careful not to touch any of the areas where the acid had burned him. Before the rest of the rioters could make a move, Natalia had thrown the assailant and the acolyte through the opening into the palace and slid back inside herself.

The rest of her loyalists slammed the door shut, and before they could pile the barricade back against the entrance, Natalia placed her palm upon the crack that separated the two doors. Taking a deep breath, she closed her eyes and drew on the last of her strength, pushing it out into her palm. The metal grew hot, and molten gold dripped onto the floor as she melted the two doors shut.

Stumbling backwards, Natalia all but collapsed into Helena's arms, her vision blurring as she gasped for breath. She was losing, and she didn't have any idea why.

S oft, warm, comforting. Safe.

That was how Natalia felt as she stirred in her bed.

She didn't remember falling asleep. In fact, she couldn't remotely recall going to bed. All she could remember was Helena catching her after she had scaled the palace doors, and she had a vague recollection of the Head Priestess calling her name and begging her to explain what had happened.

Opening her eyes slowly, Natalia tried to roll over and winced. Her body felt heavy, as though her limbs were filled with lead, and even the very act of breathing seemed to take a great deal of effort.

Had she really lost so much of her powers that she was now beginning to feel the effects of their use? She had *never* felt this way before. Extended use of her abilities hadn't even caused a mild headache before; it had been as natural to her as breathing itself. Everything was changing, and not for the better as far as Natalia was concerned.

With a grunt and a whimper, Natalia forced the covers off her body and sat up. She flinched as her body protested the movements, and inhaling a deep breath caused her lungs to groan like an unoiled machine as it forced itself to move despite the rust.

"My Lady, please, just relax. Your body needs to rest and recuperate. The strain of the last few days has taken its toll upon you," Helena whispered, appearing suddenly at her bedside.

There was an uncertainty in Helena's tone that Natalia didn't recognize, though she could not have argued against it being there, either. She was meant to be flawless; she was meant to be all powerful. The fight with her citizens shouldn't have caused her to collapse as it so clearly had. For a brief moment, Natalia considered reaching out to her sisters for their opinions, but her head ached enough, and she didn't have the capacity to deal with their jibes in her current condition.

Natalia turned her head to face her Head Priestess, wondering how long it would be before even her most loyal subjects began to turn away from her. She had lost Jules, and she had lost another acolyte. Funny how none of Helena's priestesses, or even the Head Priestess herself, hadn't made a move to protect her whatsoever. Had their loyalty begun to waver even before this latest incident?

"The acolyte, the one who died, what was his name?" Natalia asked, wincing as her throat scratched uncomfortably, and her tongue felt a hundred times larger than it should have been.

"I… I would have to ask the other acolytes, my Lady. I do not know," Helena answered, eyebrows raised high at the unexpected question.

"Do that," Natalia replied, closing her eyes for a moment as she lied back down, curling into a ball despite the reluctant creak of her muscles.

"I'll go and speak to them now. I will send in one of my girls with something to eat and drink," Helena said more confidently, bowing to Natalia as she hurried from the room.

Natalia listened as her footsteps hurried away. She maneuvered herself so that she could watch the woman leave, shocked to find that the doors had been re-hung on their hinges so that they could be shut once more. How long had she been asleep for?

Sitting up again, Natalia turned her head toward her windows. The glass had all been cleared from the floor, and the frames were set back into their places, though there were no new panes—instead, there was a temporary measure of wooden boards to keep them closed. It was ugly, and wouldn't allow Natalia to view herself. It was the first time since creating the world that Natalia was faced with something that *wouldn't* reflect her beauty back to her.

Part of her wanted to lie back down, pull the covers over her head, and go back to sleep for a thousand years. Maybe then, she would wake up and realize that all of this was just a horrible nightmare sent by God as His last act of punishment for proving that she was better than He was. She knew better, but the icy grip of doubt lingered in her heart, and she could hope that all of this was just a mistake.

Another part of her wanted to get up, to throw open the windows to her balcony, and see what remained of her beautiful, perfect city. But if the city was in ruins, did she really want that image to mar her sight? She could rebuild, she could make it just as it had been, but first, she had to deal with the slight issue of her rebellious citizens…

"That man," Natalia whispered, throwing the covers from her body and swinging her legs over the edge of her bed. "What happened to him?" she asked the empty room.

Forcing herself to her feet, Natalia gripped at one of the bed posts as her knees buckled slightly. She was exhausted, but she was *not* going to give up; she was better than this! She was the best, and she wanted *answers*.

Shuffling to her dresser, Natalia slipped her feet into the silk slippers that had found their way back to where they belonged. She threw on a light robe from her dresser chair and made her way out of her bedroom, slipping through a crack in the door that Helena had left.

"My Lady? Shouldn't you be in bed? Resting?" a female acolyte, guarding her room, asked as she appeared in the corridor.

"What happened to the rebel that I brought into the palace?" Natalia asked, ignoring the question entirely.

"Priestess Helena instructed us to lock him in the cellar, my Lady, since we don't have a dungeon to speak of," the acolyte continued, daring to look up at Natalia. "I can take you to him, if you wish."

"I do. I have questions, and I believe he may have the answers." Natalia growled.

It was time to put this nonsense to rest, once and for all.

Natalia never spent any time in the palace cellar; she had absolutely no need to, after all. Her subjects were there to cater to her every need. What possible reason would have compelled her to venture into the depths of the palace?

Funny, now the cellar had been turned into a glorified dungeon. Not only did Natalia now have to venture down into it for the first time since she created her world, but now she chastised herself for not making an *actual* dungeon when she had constructed her palace.

As if she would ever have *dreamt* of needing one! She gave her people everything they needed to survive; they lived an eternal life of luxury with everything they could ever have asked for. They only had to love her.

She would never have imagined needing to *punish* her subjects; how hard was it to worship her? They'd all managed for so many years that it had never once crossed her mind that things would change as dramatically as they had.

Now she understood why her father had created Hell for Lucifer and the others who dared to act against Him. It set an example for the rest... well, to a point. Natalia, Raziel, and Azazel seemed to be the exceptions, though Natalia believed that was because God was too afraid to even *dare* send *her* down there. She'd have released the pit onto his precious city in the clouds! Best to leave her to create her own world rather than risk irritating her and unleashing her wrath. A wise move on His part; one of the few, in her opinion.

Striding down the steps into the lower levels of the palace, Natalia followed after the acolyte, feeling oddly out of place in her own palace. She didn't belong down here in the dark, dingy depths of her home. While it was still beautiful, the walls mirrored and the floors made of shining gold as the rest of the palace was, it felt darker and colder.

Natalia didn't like it. She felt exposed in a way that made her skin crawl. She could imagine her sisters lurking in the shadows like this, but not herself; this just didn't suit her. Natalia was meant to be on display for all to see, so that they could stare at her and gasp in awe. They couldn't do that when she was hidden away in the cavernous depths of the palace cellar...

Natalia held her head high as the acolyte turned to face her, clearly looking to her to see if she was content with continuing on. The last thing she needed was for those still loyal to her to start questioning whether or not she was in her right mind, or confident in her own decisions. She would not allow them to see her falter, not now, not ever. It wasn't going to happen!

"Oh, Sister, but it already is." Azazel's pompous tone slithered into Natalia's head, and she was forced to keep her face straight, despite the disdain she felt at her sister's interruption.

"And you're faring any better, are you?" Natalia rebuked silently.

Normally, Natalia would have spoken aloud to her sibling. She had done so on numerous occasions in front of the acolytes, and they'd grown accustomed to these somewhat strange one-sided conversations. However, this time, she didn't want anyone eavesdropping on her conversation with Azazel.

Raziel's absence hadn't gone unnoticed, either, though after their last contact, Natalia was beginning to question whether their sister would join in on the taunting or not moving forward. It seemed that Raziel's grip on her world was slipping far quicker, but Natalia intended on fixing hers before it slipped any further than this minor hiccup that she was currently suffering.

"Tell me, Sister, how close have your people come to slitting your throat?" Natalia added with a smirk, flicking her curls over her shoulder as she strode after the acolyte.

"No closer than usual." Azazel snorted.

"Not that you would tell me even if they had. Oh, Sister, such bravado, but if Raziel is slipping, I know for a fact that you will, too. As if you could surpass me in keeping control."

Natalia cut the connection before her sister could utter whatever retort she may have been formulating. Natalia had won that round, naturally, and she was going to leave her sister seething at that.

"Mistress?" The acolyte turned to face Natalia, a look of concern upon the young woman's smooth featured face.

Natalia smiled at her, reaching out a hand and caressing the girl's cheeks with her fingertips. A swell of amusement rippled in Natalia's stomach as the acolyte shivered at her touch and let out a soft, whimpering moan. Humans really *were* such simple creatures. The gentlest touch, and they were putty in her hands. That brush of the cheek would keep this particular acolyte loyal for centuries, millennia even, in the hopes that Natalia would honor her with another in the future. Or something more intimate, if she was lucky. And she might be.

The girl was pretty, meek, and her skin was soft. Natalia had been considering bedding Helena, but she might take this girl instead since she was likely to appreciate that intimacy more since she didn't expect it like Helena did.

Her priestess was loyal, she couldn't deny that, but the seeds of suspicion were sown already, and Natalia questioned whether Helena was getting above her station. Especially since Jules' unfortunate demise.

Jules. The mere thought of her Head Priest caused a slight fluttering in Natalia's heart, and she made the conscious effort *not* to scowl at this unexpected and unfamiliar feeling. The man had been by her side from the very beginning; he'd been the most devoted from the moment she'd chosen him to come to her world. In fact, Jules had been the first human she picked to be amongst her citizens. How she had forgotten that, she didn't know. Then again, it hadn't seemed that important at the time.

What did it matter who was picked when? Was Helena second? Was that where their rivalry for her time and affection had begun? Why *now* did she feel Jules' missing presence more than she believed she would? He was only a human, but he *had* been particularly devoted to her, and given the nonsense that was currently going on in her world, she would've liked him by her side. Natalia hadn't realized how much she'd come to rely upon the man, or how normal it was for him to be beside her, until he wasn't.

These rebels would pay. She was going to create them their own very special Hell, just as her father had. They would suffer punishments that even *she* would shiver at, all because they'd turned against her and taken Jules from her. *Her* Head Priest, the man she'd appointed as her speaker for the people so that they would be *closer* to her through one of their own.

No, she would not forgive that slight, nor the fact that they had meant to harm *her* with the acid that had ruined poor Jules' beautiful face. They would all suffer at her hands, and then they would come to realize just how good they'd had it beforehand… and they would beg on their knees for her to forgive them. All of them.

Several acolytes and priestesses hurried to the numerous doors that lined the corridors in the deepest depths of the palace as the rumor spread of Natalia's presence in their domain. They bowed as she passed, their whispers preceding her arrival, and following after her as she swept past them.

She could feel their surprise, palpable in the air, so thick that Natalia reckoned she could reach out and physically *touch* their emotions. They had never seen her down here, by the kitchens, and rightly so. Why in her name would she ever need to be down here, where her subjects worked for her? This was their domain within her world, not hers, though there was a thought that maybe Natalia should surprise them more often. Their shock and awe were a delightfully sweet treat on her tongue, and just the salve her heavy heart needed after all that had gone on recently. They loved her, they *loved her*, and they were grateful for this minor glance of their goddess.

Yes. She would grace her humble servants with her physical presence more often—not too often, though, or else the anticipation and shock would be lost, and the joy at this glimpse of her would be faded. But she would come down more than she did before, which wouldn't be hard considering that she'd never been.

Passing the last of the kitchen doors, there loomed a colossal door of pure gold. The mirrored surface was polished to perfection, as the entire palace was, so Natalia could still look upon her own magnificence as she caught her reflection.

However, there were no engraved depictions of herself. No sculpted scenes of her dancing or lounging under the sun. Natalia had never thought to grace any decoration on this end of the palace, because she'd never expected to *be* here.

The acolyte hurried to one of the huge ring handles, throwing her entire weight backwards to shift the massive door, with no success whatsoever. Natalia stepped forward, waving the girl away with a dismissive hand and a slight smirk. She took hold of the handle with one hand and pulled.

When the door did not immediately give way to her natural strength, which should have allowed her to open the cellar entrance with minimal effort on her part, Natalia scowled. If it had not been for her reflection scowling back at her, Natalia might have left the expression on her face, but she could see the acolyte staring at her and did not need the girl to notice Natalia's confusion. With a shake of her head,

Natalia tried again, putting more force behind her movement this time.

The door gave way with no further protest this time, and Natalia felt her muscles relax in her shoulders. She hadn't even realized how tense she had become; she just hoped that the acolyte hadn't noticed it, either. With Jules gone, the acolytes would turn to Helena, and the *last* thing Natalia wanted was for word to get back to the Head Priestess that their goddess was not in her right mind. Helena would come fishing, and the more Natalia thought about the woman, the more Natalia wanted to keep Helena at arm's length.

Natalia opened the door just wide enough for her to fit through. She had no idea what precautions the others had taken to secure and restrain their prisoner, and she was not about to let him escape... not until she was done with him, anyway.

"Stay here and guard the door. I will call for you if I need you," Natalia instructed the acolyte, her eyes fixed on the dimly flickering light that beckoned to her from the below.

"B-but Mistress!" the acolyte squeaked in protest.

Natalia stepped closer to the girl, her lip curling unpleasantly. The acolyte whimpered and jumped backwards. Throwing herself, prostrate, to the ground as she trembled under Natalia's dark gaze.

Satisfied that the girl had been thoroughly rebuked, Natalia turned back to the doorway, slipping inside and making her way gracefully down the stairs that led to the lowest part of the palace. Torches flickered and glowed on the walls, reflecting off the gleaming golden surfaces like a million fireflies captured in glass jars, though they offered little to no warmth this deep under the ground.

A shiver ran up Natalia's spine as the cold began to seep into her feet, digging icy claws into her very bones despite the silk slippers that she had put on before leaving her bedroom. They may as well have not existed, but Natalia knew they would at least protect her from damaging her perfect skin on the freezing golden floors.

The stairs spiraled down, down, down, deep into the darkness, and for a moment, Natalia wondered if she *had* in fact created her own Hell within her world, until finally, the stairs ended, and the cellar opened out to greet her.

There was no loving embrace waiting for her at the bottom, no gasps of admiration or sighs of adulation. No one sobbed for joy at being in her presence, nor proclaimed their love for her. No. All that waited at the bottom was a cavernous room filled with supplies that blocked out what little light the torches offered, casting monstrous shadows around her as a cold breeze whipped across her slender, perfect frame, snatching at her hair and clothes as it left her chilled to her core.

Laughter rang out from the other end of the room, reverberating off the walls as it finally reached her. It wasn't a joyous sound, and it didn't bring any lightness to Natalia's heart. In fact, it brought back that doubt that she had been denying existed. A vice-like grip took hold of her heart as her eyes searched through the shadows for the source of the almost maniacal laughter, until finally, she spotted her prisoner.

On his knees, wrapped in chains that looked heavy enough to break his back, the man watched her with mad eyes, and a look of pure hatred on his face. The smile was one she hadn't seen in eons, and only once when she had faced Lucifer with the rest of her army. It was a smile that spoke volumes about the hatred that her brother had felt for their father and those who had (at the time) supported what their father stood for. Never in all of her days would Natalia have *ever* believed that someone could look at her in the same way, as though faced with some foul demon spawn that had no right to exist.

Anger rose in her heart at the expression. He should have loved her! That was his purpose in her world, to worship the ground she walked on, the very air that they shared! She gave them the gifts of eternal life, of easy living, and all she'd asked in return was their love. And yet, here he knelt, *daring* to think badly of her?!

Natalia stepped toward the man with purpose, ready to strike him when he laughed again, the sound so jarring that it stopped even *her* in her tracks.

"So, the *mighty goddess* has deemed me worthy of an audience, has she? How lucky I must be to get to speak to her alone. Don't expect an apology from me, nor the admiration you *think* should be yours. I don't cower to false gods, nor do I show praise to ugly things like you."

The man's words stung as though he had just struck Natalia against the face. Natalia took a step away from her prisoner, taken aback by his words. No one had ever dared speak to her in such a fashion other than her siblings, and the only reason she allowed it from *them* was because they were closer to her in status. They would never be on par with her, admittedly, but at least they were higher beings whom she could tolerate such nonsense from.

This man was human, an *insect* in comparison to a divine being such as herself. Natalia was an *angel*. Fallen or otherwise, it made no difference. She had been created by God himself, by the Creator!

Laughter bit at her ears, and Natalia scowled as the man seemed to enjoy her hesitation. The sound of his voice was an insult to her existence, and she was tempted to pull his head clean from his shoulders right then and there, and she would have done it if she hadn't wanted to speak with him about what was happening.

"No one has ever told you no before, have they?" He snorted, smirking at her.

Natalia snorted in return, not deeming it necessary to give him a response as she crossed the cellar, standing over him with her arms crossed over her ample bosom. At this angle, he was forced to lean back, the chains clinking, weighing heavily upon his shoulders as he attempted to meet her gaze. It was Natalia's turn to smirk this time, grinning contentedly at the fact that he was clearly uncomfortable and in pain in the position he was currently sitting in.

"I'm assuming this isn't just a social call?" The man sighed, a clear attempt at keeping what little control he had, which as far as *she* was concerned, was none whatsoever.

"I want answers," she replied curtly.

"And what makes you think I'm going to be the one to give them to you?"

Natalia's fingers dug into her arms as she forced herself not to react to his tone, too similar to Azazel's for her liking, but she would not rise to his taunts. She was far better than that.

"Oh. Are you going to *make* me?" He chortled.

Natalia hissed, unable to ignore his tone any longer since it was a *direct* insult against her. A red mist descended over her eyes as she untangled her arms and swept one hand through the air, backhanding the man straight across his face. She hit him with such force that the slap let out a *snap* that echoed across the room.

She'd propelled him to one side, and the chains clinked

and clunked as he fell heavily against the ground with a grunt of pain. There was a light amongst the darkness, threatening to overtake her mood at the sound of his agony, knowing that she'd at *least* managed to do him some damage, even if his personality was as stubborn as hers was.

Striding to where he had fallen, Natalia knelt beside him, gripped his chains, and pulled him upright until his face was mere millimeters from her own. She could almost *taste* his breath on her tongue as he panted, but at least there was a modicum of fear in his expression now that she'd given a further show of her strength.

"Do you really believe that I don't have the capability to make you talk, should I wish for it?"

"No, I don't." He shook his head.

The answer was *not* what Natalia had been expecting, and she could see her own surprise reflected back at her in his deep brown eyes.

"Nothing you can do to me will make me tell you anything. Pain is fleeting, and will only eventually lead to my death. You'll kill me out of frustration before you can force me to speak to you."

"Given that I can gift you eternal life, what makes you think I couldn't inflict centuries of pain upon you before you would even come *close* to dying?" Natalia hissed, smiling softly as she thought about how much pleasure she would get from hurting those who dared to insult her in this fashion.

"You really don't see it, do you?" the man asked. This time, it appeared that it was his turn to be astonished by something she'd said.

"See what?!" she snapped.

"You don't. You don't see it!" He laughed.

Natalia snarled and stood up, his chains still gripped in one hand as she lifted him from the floor, his feet dangling as she fought the urge to cut off his windpipe.

"See what?" She snarled once more.

"Your powers are dwindling, Great Goddess. They have been for some time now; we've all seen it, out in your great city. Places where your powers are starting to lose their hold on the world, where the gold stops gleaming and turns to plain brick, where people have grown old and *died* a natural death rather than suffering for all eternity at your feet. You don't even know it's happening because you've locked yourself up here, in your golden palace, and stared at your own reflection thinking you're perfect and beautiful. Well, I *will* tell you this. You can know all of this for free because *nothing* would give me greater pleasure than to tear you down from your pedestal and bring you back down to Earth with the rest of us. You are not beautiful; you are not loved. You are rotten to the core, black and hollow and ugly on the inside, and it shows through that porcelain face of yours. We all see it; we see through your façade to the putrid being that you really are. No one will ever truly love you; it's all a lie that you tell yourself, but I can promise you that *no one* will love you no matter what you do. You can punish us all you like, but you cannot win this. We will rise against you and bring you down. It's inevitable."

"No!" Natalia screamed, throwing the man away from herself as though he'd burned her fingers.

He grunted as his shoulder collided with the floor, but Natalia derived no pleasure from it this time. He was wrong; he was *wrong*! He *had* to be.

"Liar!" she screamed the accusation. Closing in on him, her finger pointed so close to his face that as he blinked, she could feel the gentle brush of his eyelashes against the tip of her finger, soft spidery kisses against her skin.

"You can deny it all you want, but they're the answers you were seeking, aren't they? Why have we turned against you?

That was what you were going to ask me, right?" he added in a pompous tone.

It was so much like Azazel, so self-righteous. Natalia glared at him, her eyes narrowed as though expecting to see her sister leave the man's body under her forceful gaze. She wouldn't have put it past her sibling in the slightest, finding a way to possess one of her subjects in order to torment her.

No, Azazel wouldn't have been able to break into her world, physically or spiritually. The only reason they could directly communicate with one another was because of their biological makeup, and the fact that they would always be in tune with one another in that way. No, her sister didn't have the strength or the wherewithal to pull off such a feat, not against *her*, anyway. In Raziel's world, maybe, but not hers.

Natalia turned away from the man, hands clutched at her chest as her heart beat painfully within. None of this was right; none of it! It couldn't be happening, not to her. She was perfect! She was the best of those wretched angels, and they'd all known it for millennia! Look at what she had created, what she had achieved on her own.

Yet, there was no way that Natalia could deny the events of the last month or so. How long had it been since everything had started to feel off? As though her world was tilted slightly to one side so that nothing could remain where it was meant to. The passage of time had never been her forte. She never took into account the days that passed, too busy basking in her own brilliance to be bothered about how *long* anything really was. It had never mattered... until now.

"The goddess isn't as perfect as she thought she was, is she?" Her tormentor sneered.

Her tormentor. Ironic, considering how she'd come down here with every intention of tormenting *him*. No. No, no, no, no...

"No!" she squealed angrily, stomping her foot so hard on the floor that she created a large crater in her wake.

She wanted to turn around and gloat at what she'd done, to show the man that she was just as strong and powerful as she had ever been, but the reality was far from it. If Natalia had been at full strength when she'd thrown this little tantrum, the entire palace would have been in danger of splitting into two, or falling into a hole where she'd made the impact.

The dent was impressive, by human standards, and would possibly strike fear into her captive, but it only proved his point. Just like the door. She should have been able to rip the stupid thing off its hinges with her little finger, but she'd had to *think* about opening it in order to actually make it move.

What was happening to her? To *them*? She assumed it was happening to the others as well; it would explain Raziel's issues and her absence from teasing Natalia lately. There was something going on, and all of them were losing ground. Azazel could lie all she wanted, but if Raziel was struggling, and Natalia was also, then there was no way that their other sibling was holding it together, as much as she would like them to believe she was—though Natalia doubted that her sister thought much of the threat against her life, given the world that Azazel had created all wanted to kill her long before now. That was just normality where Azazel's world was concerned, but not in Natalia's.

"No!" Natalia whined, slumping to the floor and scowling. She pulled her knees up to her chest and rested her chin upon them, her bottom lip jutting out as she pouted in frustration. All she'd ever wanted was for people to realize how amazing she was. How was that too much to ask for?

"You really have never been told no, have you?" the man mused, chains clinking as he shifted his weight to look at her better.

"Well, that's clearly not the case. Otherwise, I'd be up *there* and not down *here*." Natalia spat, pointing first to the ceiling, and then to the floor, indicating Heaven and Earth.

"Alright, touché, fair point. My bad." The man sighed. "But *other* than God, no one has ever really told you no or contradicted you, have they?"

"Again, not the case. You seem to think you know me, *little man*, but you know nothing about me whatsoever." Natalia sniffed.

"John."

"What?"

"My name is John. Not that you care, but it's my name."

"You're right, I *don't* care," Natalia replied haughtily.

"So, since I clearly don't know anything about you, why don't you tell me?"

"Tell you *what*?" Natalia snapped, fed up with listening to John's voice. He was so sanctimonious that it was nauseating.

"Well, you've said I don't know you, so why don't you tell me about yourself? It's your favorite subject after all, right?"

Again, there was that pompous, smirking tone to his voice that left Natalia wanting to rip his throat out with her bare hands. The problem was he did know *that* much about her at least, and even she couldn't deny that.

Yes. She was her own favorite subject, and the idea of being able to talk about herself was always appealing. Though this was the first time she would have spoken to anyone, Jules and Helena included, about the aspects of her life prior to building this world.

"Why do you want to know?" Natalia sulked, the prospect of being able to talk at *length* about herself still not quite enough to drag her from the mire of doubt she now found herself in.

She'd been denying what was going on in her world for as long as she could, and now that she was confronted with the reality of it, she wasn't happy. Natalia had spent her entire existence believing that she was the most powerful and flawless being in the Universe. And this small, insignificant human being was proving otherwise.

It was a dark thought, all-consuming and dangerous. She wanted to weep, scream, and feel nothing all at once. Her world was shattering around her, and it wasn't God or even another angel taking it from her; it was this *lesser* thing.

John sighed and rolled his eyes. "Well, it's not like I've got anything better to do right now, and I can't stand the thought of you sitting here having a tantrum for however long. So, I'd rather you talked about yourself and prove your point to me than have me witness a grown woman acting like a toddler."

Natalia raised her head from her knees, staring at John in utter disbelief. Never in her life would she have expected a human to speak to her in such a fashion, and still, he had the *nerve* to say it without hesitation or fear of punishment.

"Fine. I'll tell you everything about myself, then you'll see, then you'll understand why I'm the best of them, why I am *perfect.*"

"I'll be the judge of that." John snorted, eliciting another infuriated screech from Natalia.

If she managed not to kill the man before she'd convinced him that she was infallible, it would be a miracle.

"So, you're just a spoiled brat then?" John had laughed after Natalia told him her life story.

"I am NOT a spoiled brat! Did you even listen to a word I've said? I've had to show those ignorant fools every day of my life that I'm better than they are, that they were beneath me. Gabriel and the others were always father's favorites, and yet I knew I was far more capable than ANY of them. He never gave me a chance, too busy fawning over those idiotic boys. None of them were ever as good as I was, as I AM. Don't you see? Look at the world I've created! Look at my perfection."

"You still don't get it, do you? This isn't perfect. It's far from it. Your view of the world has blinded you to the reality that even YOU are not infallible, neither is God if He's made angels like you. You all look down on us as though we are the flawed creatures. Throughout history, we're taught about the angels judging whether or not WE are worthy of the existence given to us. But you're no better than we are! You're just as imperfect, just as easily led, just as naïve and stubborn. It's hypocrisy, that we're meant to be mortals while you're seen as divine. There's nothing divine about you. You're just humans with wings and a ridiculously long lifespan."

"I'm immortal."

"Snap all you like, but you know I'm right. You really aren't any better than I am, and you wonder why we hate living in this world that you've created? You think we should all bow down to you and worship you because you're beautiful, and outwardly you are, but there is so much more to life than just looks. Have you ever looked at another person and seen them for who they are? For what strengths they may have? No, because your head is so far up your own—"

"Be careful what you say to me, human."

"Your own ego is so big that you haven't realized that true perfection is found in imperfection. There's an old saying, 'light shines through the cracks of a vase.' In other words, the TRULY beautiful things shine through that which isn't perfect. Those of us who are broken, flawed humans, we're the beautiful ones. We're the ones who find strength no matter what. We're unique, and we see the true images of those around us because we can see what's INSIDE a person, not just what's on the outside. That's why I can never love you the way you want, because I already love someone else, someone who is more beautiful than you could EVER be to me. Do you even know what that's like?

To really love someone, to feel that devoted to someone else?"

The exchange went round and round in Natalia's head as she lied on her bed and stared at the canopy above her. She hated how much he had gotten into her head, how his words stung as though he had repeatedly slapped her across the face.

They didn't love her. They didn't love the world that she had created for them. Apparently, they'd come to hate her gift of immortality. It hadn't felt that long since she'd created this world, but John had alluded that the passage of centuries had grown tiresome on the humans she had hand-picked to live in this utopia.

"How can flaws be a good thing?" She hissed, fists punching the duvet beneath her. "How can he say that they *like* imperfections?! Don't they *constantly* strive for things to be perfect?!" she screamed, sitting up sharply as she stared at the empty chamber.

Not so long ago, Jules would have come running into the room to see if his beloved Mistress was alright, willing to do anything to make her happy again. *Why* did she keep thinking of the man?! He was dead; he was inconsequential; he was…

"He was mine," Natalia muttered, pulling her knees up to her chest and hugging her arms around them.

She'd never thought about him that way before, not in that sense, anyway. That bloody John had gotten into her head alright; he was leaving her with strange thoughts, and she didn't like it one bit.

"Did you love him?"

Natalia gasped, spinning around on the bed, expecting to find her sister sitting behind her, but of course, Raziel wasn't *actually* there. However, her presence was so much stronger now than it had ever been. Natalia could *feel* her sister—not just hear her—just as she'd been able to when they'd been in Heaven and apart. Their connection was growing stronger; did that mean that their barriers were growing weaker? If John's words were true, that might explain it.

"Who?" Natalia asked.

"The one who died for you. The priest, or whatever he was."

"Do you even care?"

"No. Yes. I don't know. You know, I've searched for love for a long time, to feel what the rest of you feel. I just wanted to know if that's what you felt for him."

"I… I don't know." Natalia scowled as she admitted this to her sister. She hadn't thought about it; she hadn't even *considered* that she might have loved Jules. She loved herself. No one else was on par with her in terms of beauty or majesty, so why would she have ever lowered herself to feeling such a thing for someone else? Jules had loved *her*, and rightly so, but loving him? "Maybe. Sort of? I don't really know. I never thought about it."

Was *that* why she kept thinking about him? About his absence from her life now? He had given his life for her, which Natalia had expected, but he should never have crossed her mind ever again after that. Replaced by another servant who gave her the attention she so desired and deserved. But he hadn't been forgotten, hadn't been passed over in her mind. She kept *looking* for him, despite knowing that he wasn't there anymore, knowing that he would *never* be there again.

Something wet tickled her cheek, and Natalia reached a hand to her face, touching the tears that blurred her vision unbidden, unexpected. Maybe she *had* loved Jules, in some way, even if it wasn't the love that Raziel was searching so desperately for. But Natalia had clearly felt *something* for her priest. Otherwise, she wouldn't keep thinking about him; she wouldn't miss him as much as she clearly did.

"Yes… I think I did, somehow," she muttered.

"So, what now?"

"I don't know."

Natalia shivered, shuffling herself under her covers and pulling them tightly around her. Her world felt cold and empty for the first time since she'd created this place. Raziel's presence vanished, and Natalia wished that her sister had remained a little longer, if only so she didn't have to be alone with her thoughts. She didn't want to be alone; she didn't want to think about what John had said to her. She didn't want to think about how Jules wasn't there for her anymore.

She didn't want to be alone.

Sleep seemed to avoid Natalia once again. She spent the night tossing and turning in her bed, her thoughts a constant rolling tsunami. She actually *missed* Jules; she *felt* his absence. Not only that, but she could not deny that she was losing her grip on her world now.

No matter what she did, there was no denying that her powers were growing weaker. The evidence of it had been right there, but she didn't want to admit to it. The fact that her people were rebelling against her, that they attacked her palace, her inability to open the door to the cellar with just one hand. None of this should have been happening! If she was truly as strong as she'd believed, then none of this would have occurred at all.

Helena came into her room in the middle of the night to inform her that the rebels remained on the steps of the palace, but there had been something else that the priestess *hadn't* said. Natalia noticed it, but she wasn't ready to hear what *else* was evidence to the fact that everything she'd believed about herself—from the moment of her creation—was a lie.

John said that she was truly ugly, that her beauty was only skin-deep, and that looks weren't enough. What had he meant? What more *was* there other than beauty? That was why she had picked all of *them* in the first place, because they had been the most beautiful of the humans. Not one of them was ugly, so how could John sit there and *dare* to say that what was on the outside wasn't important?

Sighing heavily, Natalia cast her covers aside and strode across the floor of her chamber to the balcony. It was a potentially foolhardy thing to do, considering the rebels camped outside her home, but she wanted the fresh air, and she wanted to look out over her city and remember it in all the glory that she had created it in.

Natalia's eyes scanned the horizon, and she gasped, her heart sinking in her chest, her stomach twisting at the sight beyond the boundary of the palace. The city was in disarray! Smoke rose into the clear blue morning sky, creating dark clouds that spoke volumes of the mood of the world she had once called hers. The rebels had torn down her statues and defaced much of the golden streets, but that wasn't the worst of it. In fact, Natalia had expected this level of vandalism from the rebels; what she hadn't expected was the rest of the destruction.

The polished gold that had lined every street dripped in great, sticky globs of sickly molten metal, leaving behind the ugly brick face of the building beneath, the *true* building that had been there before she had come along and reshaped it to her liking.

Natalia hurried to the edge of the balcony, gripping the golden railing as she leaned over to see just how far the devastation ran. The palace was intact, though even Natalia could see that the sheen to it had dulled. There was a distinct line that could be seen where the city was returning to the ugly, tedious origins from before Natalia had tenderly sculpted it into a beacon of glorious perfection.

"Mistress! Come away from there. It's dangerous!" Helena cried out.

Natalia charged for the priestess, all thoughts of mercy long gone as she all but flew to the woman's side, hand outstretched as she gripped Helena's throat tightly in one hand.

"When were you going to tell me about this?!" Natalia screeched, waving a hand at the city beyond, her eyes drawn to the gray concrete buildings that stood instead of the beautiful gold ones that she had created.

"Mistress, I—" Helena gasped and stammered under the pressure of Natalia's grip.

"You have been lying to me! How long have you been plotting against me? Did *you* help Samuel into the Throne Room? Or were you the one who helped that man get into my *bedroom*? Was it jealousy that caused you to do it? Because I was ready to finally take Jules to my bed, so you sent that man to hurt us? Is that what happened?!"

"No! Never!" Helena wept.

There was a sincerity in the priestesses' words that even Natalia could not deny, not that it made her feel any better. Natalia screamed with frustration as she relinquished her grip on the woman, turning her back on the priestess as she stared out at the city. She closed her eyes, ignoring the gasping and sobbing behind her, as she held her hands out in front of her and concentrated.

This was *her* world. No one was going to take it from her, or tell her any differently. She was going to reclaim it. Take it back, rebuild it, and regain control of *all* her citizens. She was going to prove these insignificant little insects wrong; she *was* infallible, and this was *her* world!

She felt her powers gathering in her very core. A soft, warm pressure deep in her stomach that began to grow, like a seed flourishing in the soil until it blossomed into a huge oak tree. The tips of her fingers began to tingle. Her skin was alive with prickling electricity as the fire of her powers engulfed her from within. At the height of her power, Natalia let out a grunt, casting it from her body like a wave that rippled across the city.

Opening her eyes, Natalia smiled to herself, anticipating that the results had worked... but it hadn't. The city remained as it had, the golden glory gone and replaced with the ugly brick and concrete shapes that she'd never expected to see again. Natalia collapsed, the cold floor stinging against her aching knees where she had connected with the unforgiving wood. It was all falling apart. Everything about this was wrong, and she couldn't stop it.

She'd accused Helena of betraying her, though she still suspected that the priestess was up to something. Natalia may not have hit the right subject, but there was still *something* going on, unless it was literally *this* that Helena had been keeping a secret. How long had the woman known that this was going on? Were she and Jules more aware of Natalia's slip in powers than they'd let on, or was it that they'd found out and kept it quiet for Natalia's sake? What *was* it?! Why was *everything* falling apart? What had she done to deserve this?

Natalia gripped her throat tightly, her breath short and

labored. Her skin was prickling again, but it wasn't the same as when she'd been building up her powers. No, this was something new, something she had never experienced before. The world grew dark, and the last thing Natalia remembered was Helena's panicked voice calling out her name, her actual name that no one other than her sisters had ever uttered before… before everything went cold and black.

When Natalia woke up, she found herself tucked into her bed, just as she had been after she'd collapsed while fighting the rebels at the door of her palace. It *was* true. She was growing weaker, and it was happening more quickly now that she'd stopped denying that it was happening at all. The covers felt like weights against her chest, restraining her against the mattress so that she couldn't move, let alone get up.

Deep down, Natalia knew that wasn't the case at all, but that was how she felt. If she couldn't keep hold of her world, if her powers were of no use to her anymore, then what was the point? Why should she even bother to get up and fight anymore? Was it even worth forcing her aching, useless body up from the safety of her bed?

The doubt that her sisters had sown after Samuel's attack on her. Samuel's words about *why* he had attacked her in the first place... That had been the spark that set the fire, that little hole in her self-assured confidence that turned into a gaping wound and let the fear and confusion into her mind, causing her to hesitate and misstep in ways she hadn't since... ever.

Natalia didn't know what to do now. All she'd ever known was her own power and beauty, but even *that* had been torn in two, and she was left feeling like an empty shell of her former self. Like she was *nothing*. She'd never felt like this before; it was a foreign, terrifying feeling. Even *that* was new. Even against the hordes of Hell, Natalia hadn't been afraid. She'd stood beside her brothers and sisters, ready to face the demon spawns and die if necessary. Not that she'd expected to die; she was too strong for such a fate... or so she'd believed.

"Mistress?" Helena's voice spoke softly, the woman's tone less sure than Natalia was used to from her priestess.

Clearly, Natalia threatening her life had shaken the woman, and rightly so. At least Natalia had managed *that* correctly, since it appeared that she was losing her grip on everything *else* that she'd once been so convinced about.

"Mistress, the rebels are at our door. My priestesses and the acolytes are struggling to keep them from breaching the barricade. I don't know how much longer the palace will be safe. We need to think of a plan, an alternative to this."

"Did you know?" Natalia muttered, ignoring the priestess' soft plea.

"Did I...?"

"About what was happening to my city, what was happening to me," Natalia accused, turning her head slowly toward the woman, her eyes utterly emotionless and a reflection of how she felt inside at that moment.

"I… we…," Helena stammered.

"Jules knew, didn't he?"

Helena stared at her hands, anything other than the soul-searching gaze that Natalia was boring into the priestess with.

"He did. We both did. We found evidence of the—of *your* —weakening in parts of the city that were furthest from the palace. We took note of the places where your beautiful city was dissolving, and marked and recorded it privately. Jules wanted to tell you, but I insisted that we say nothing, that we would silently find a way to fix the problem for you without you ever knowing. I meant no offense, no harm, I just…," Helena whimpered, fingers gripping at the duvet that kept Natalia contained for the moment.

"Thank you," Natalia whispered.

"M-mistress?!" Helena gasped.

Never, in all their time together, had Natalia *thanked* any of her subjects for *anything*, not with any real sincerity, anyway. Yet, now she had, and it was no surprise that it shocked Helena to hear it.

"Did you do it because you love me, or you think you love me, because you wanted to make me happy? Or was it because you didn't want to see me angry? Maybe it's fear, not love," Natalia muttered, remembering what John had said to her before.

"My Lady…," Helena interrupted, getting up to sit on the edge of the bed so that she could be closer to Natalia as she spoke, her hand hovering over the duvet as though she was debating holding her Mistress' hand, but wasn't sure if she should or not. After a second, Helena chose to rest her hand on the duvet, close to Natalia's body without actually touching her. "It was always love for me, *and* for Jules. The reason he and I fought was because, out of all your subjects, we were the ones who were closest to you, and we were the ones who knew everything. We still loved you, my Lady, Jules more than myself, even I have to admit. I know you picked up on our rivalry, and it was because I was jealous of him. You always seemed closer to Jules than to me, spending more time in his company than my own, despite his meek attitude around you. And that was only because he loved you so much that he grew nervous around you, but he *did* love you with all his heart, a truer love than I could ever claim to have."

Helena sighed heavily, staring at her hands, still unable to meet Natalia's eyes as she spoke. "If I had been here when that man attacked you, I would *like* to think that I would have pushed you out of the way and taken the attack myself, but... the thought of it fills me with fear, and I cannot say that I would have done what he did. We knew you were losing your powers, or at least, they were growing weaker in some fashion, but we loved you so much that we wanted to ensure you knew nothing about it. We wanted to fix it for you *because* of our love for you. I'm just sorry we couldn't do more." Helena sighed.

Warmth spread through Natalia's body, making her feel less empty and more like herself. Filled with renewed energy —though not entirely recovered, by any means—just enough to feel a little better, Natalia sat up slowly, reaching out to take Helena's hand.

"Do what you can to deal with the rebels at our door, but no further than that. I'm going to speak to our prisoner again and see if we can find a way around this. I am still in charge of this world; I am still the goddess here, and I will *not* let them get away with this."

Helena smiled and nodded. "As you wish, my Lady."

Natalia watched the priestess leave the room, taking a

moment to catch her breath before she cast aside the duvet cover. She needed to figure out how to put a stop to all of this. She needed to keep her palace and those still loyal to her safe from the rebels on their doorstep. And she had a feeling that the man in the depths of her cellar might have the answers she was looking for... again.

"So, she graces me with her presence yet again. I *must* be special." John snorted as Natalia padded her way, bare-footed, across the freezing cellar floor to where he was still chained up.

Natalia rolled her eyes as she stood over him, her hands on her hips. Helena had sent her a couple of priestesses to help her get dressed in an attempt to make Natalia feel more like herself, which she had to admit, she did. A little, at least. It was amazing what a good bath, some flattering clothes, and someone brushing her hair until it shone like marble could do to chase away the looming rain clouds in a person's mind.

"According to you, everyone's special in their own right, just not me!" Natalia snapped.

"Not entirely what I said, though I'm surprised you listened to me at all. So, that's something. What brings the *mighty* goddess down to the depths to see little old me?" John asked, sitting back, his chains clinking with every movement.

"I wanted to ask you how we can resolve all of this. How we can work to stop the rebels before anyone else gets hurt."

John stared up at her, blinking rapidly, his mouth partially open. Natalia smiled wickedly and chuckled, hands clasped behind her back as she leaned forward slightly, her breasts pushed forward as she tilted her head to one side.

"Speechless? I didn't think it was possible!" She laughed.

Natalia flicked out her skirt and settled onto the cold floor in front of him, crossing her legs and placing her hands in her lap as she watched John carefully, amused as he smirked at her words.

"Alright, you win that round. But do you mean it? Do you *actually* mean you want to fix things?" he asked her.

"I cannot deny my nature. I know my worth, I know what I'm capable of, and I *know* that I am the best at what I do and cannot believe otherwise. That is not to say I could not become *more* perfect by listening. You've said to me that there is inner beauty, that a person is not just about how they look, but how they *are.* That you fell in love with a woman in my world, not *just* because she was beautiful outside, but as a person. What was it? A cracked vase shines with light from within?"

"That's right," John replied, sitting up straight and leaning toward Natalia as he let her speak without interruption.

Natalia noticed the absence of any snide remarks from the man, having grown used to listening to him laugh or snap back at her.

"If I can adjust, if I can be more… forgiving and a little less… me, would you all stay? Would that stop the rebels?"

"You would change the world and let us love one another? Like *truly* love one another?"

Natalia scowled a little, her fingers automatically moving to massage the wrinkles that formed on her face so that they would not become permanent.

"I… yes. That's what I'm thinking. I want my priestesses and acolytes to be safe, and if what you say is true, then maybe I have missed out on a type of love and worship that is deeper than what you have all shown me so far."

"The word you're looking for is respect." John smirked, returning to his old self.

"I would still expect you all to worship me. I *am* still your goddess, after all." She grunted in return. "But I would be willing to let you lead more normal lives, what you had prior to my choosing you all to be mine."

"Why the sudden change of heart?" John asked, narrowing his gaze at her.

"My powers have been weakening, as you've so clearly pointed out, and I am looking to rectify the issue. The only reason I can think of for the sudden loss in my powers, is purely because I've grown lax in my own growth. I'm an angel. We trained regularly to ensure that we were ready for war against the spawn of Hell, and I've allowed myself to become negligent."

"Is that the *only* reason?" John urged.

Natalia felt her heart twist in her chest, as though someone had grasped it with both hands and turned them in the opposite direction from one another, screwing it around and leaving her gasping for breath. She looked away from the man, unsure of how to answer his question. The niggling doubt returned, that unsure feeling that left her feeling cold and sick because it felt so strange and unfamiliar. Slick and oil-like, tendrils of uncertainty slithering their way into her mind.

"No," Natalia admitted, pushing the feeling away and swallowing hard. "John… how did you know you were in love?"

"How did I…?" John repeated, blinking at Natalia as he had when she'd offered the potential for a new world, under a slightly different regime. "You think you're in love with someone? The priest?"

"I… I don't know. I find myself thinking about him, about how much I miss him, and my stomach twists, and my heart hurts. He gave his life for me, and I thought I'd expected it of him because I *wanted* you all to love me, but I wish he hadn't. I keep wanting to wake up and find him waiting outside my bedroom door to greet me as he always did, with his eyes down and trying not to look at me because he's too nervous to look me in the eyes. I never realized how much he was there for me, how often I would turn to him for the smallest things—"

"Until he wasn't there anymore, and you realized you would do anything to have him back?" John asked.

"Y-yes."

"That's love. It's hard to explain, but for someone like yourself, someone *so* caught up in their own worth, I would say you found true love."

Natalia's bottom lip quivered, and she hugged her knees to her chest, resting her chin on her knees as her vision blurred, and she felt the tears trickle down her cheeks. She'd loved him; she really had. For the first time in her existence, she'd loved something, some*one* other than herself, and now, he was gone forever.

"How do I live without him?" she whimpered.

John leaned backwards, as though her words had struck him in the chest in the same way as her fist might have. He was clearly taken aback by her question, and the look in his eyes told her that he didn't have the answer to that, and that no one would. Jules was gone. She couldn't bring him back; that wasn't in her sphere of abilities, and now she was going to have to live with that for the rest of eternity.

Wiping the tears from her eyes, Natalia stood up and brushed the dust from her skirt and her legs, righting her clothes as a way of gathering her composure before she went back into the palace proper.

"If I approach the rebels with the proposition of a new world, one where they can love one another so long as they still pay worship to me and appreciate all that I have given to them, will they stop their assault on the palace?" she asked sternly.

"Yes, I think they would. I can't guarantee that it will be easy, or that they will love you in the way that you want them to, but they would be happier and more willing if you allowed them more freedom." John nodded. "If you could see them for who they are, you might find more people who can touch your heart like Jules did. There're all kinds of love, my Lady, and all of them can bring happiness to you if you let them."

Natalia turned away and strode toward the steps, her heart pounding painfully in her chest as she made a decision about her future… and that of her world.

"We shall see."

Compromise. That was what she was considering right now. *Compromise.*

Natalia had never compromised anything in her entire life! That had contributed to her fall, and she hated it! Her unwavering faith in herself, her love of her own beauty and powers, her strength and bravery and self-assured confidence in everything she did, were the only things she ever relied on. Yet all of that was being torn away from her, and now she wasn't just considering compromise, but she was *willing* to.

How did it even come to this?

"Helena?" Natalia called softly to her priestess as she

hugged herself in her bed, pulling her duvet up to her chin and shivering despite not being cold.

"My Lady?" The woman hurried through the bedroom door to her bedside, a look of concern on her face at Natalia's dejected tone.

"Can you run me a bath?" Natalia asked as Helena settled on the edge of the bed, offering her hand, which Natalia took without question.

"Of course! Do you want all of the girls?" Helena asked, gently stroking her thumb over the back of Natalia's hand in a comforting fashion.

"No, just you. And John. Bring him up from the cellar. Give him some new clothes and something to eat."

"But my Lady!" Helena protested, freezing in her movement as she stared incredulously at her Mistress.

"Just do it for me, please."

Helena nodded, squeezed Natalia's hand, and hurried from the room, hesitating by the door to look back at her Mistress as though Natalia might come to her senses in a moment if she lingered a little longer. When it was clear that Natalia meant every word, Helena delayed no longer.

Natalia threw the covers from her body, shuffling her way to the balcony where she could see the state of her city as it continued its terrible decay. Almost all of the city had lost its golden luster now, and her statues were blobs of molten metal that were unrecognizable.

She'd noticed that even her palace was growing dimmer now, the shimmer and shine of the mirrored surfaces becoming more blurred and less beautiful. She couldn't bear to look at herself in it anymore, her images distorted and twisted because of it. A reminder that she would soon lose everything, and the rebels would breach her walls, whether she liked it or not.

She sat on the balcony, one foot hanging over the edge. It

was lucky that the stone was thick enough for her to sit on, or she would've been perilously close to falling onto the street below. To the waiting arms of the rebels, who would happily tear her limb from limb; she was sure of that.

Natalia looked down at the street, her eyes fixed on the citizens of her world who remained camped at the edge of her palace. Most of them crowded the steps to the main entrance, though a few of the more intelligent ones had begun to patrol the borders of the palace for another way in. Thankfully, the priestesses and acolytes were one step ahead of them, and any other ways inside were already barricaded to stop them from getting in... or at least slow them down enough for Natalia to come up with a plan.

She had a plan. She knew what she needed to do now, but she wanted to speak to John again first. He'd opened her eyes to new possibilities, to avenues that she and her sisters would *never* have considered before, and while she was more willing to listen now, she was still reluctant to admit that she would need to give in.

"Your bath is ready, my Lady, and your guest is on his way to the bathroom!" Helena called from the doorway.

"I'll be there in a minute, Helena. Go on without me," Natalia replied, looking over her shoulder at the priestess.

Helena hesitated before nodding and vanishing from sight once more.

Natalia sighed heavily, closing her eyes as she drew in a slow, deep breath. The world was changing, and she wasn't consciously causing it. It was unsettling. Was this how God felt when Lucifer had first rebelled? Or when the people He'd put on his Earth began to turn their faces away from him and didn't believe as heavily as they had before? Did God question his own movements?

Exhaling slowly, Natalia opened her eyes and stared up at the sky. She pictured where Heaven should be, though she didn't expect to see anything. However, the problem was that she *did* see something. Natalia scowled, swinging her legs from the edge of the balcony to stand on the floor as she leaned over the railing, staring up at the shimmering vision that shouldn't have been there.

High above her city, in the midst of the perpetual sunny sky that she'd created, was what she could only describe as a *tear* in the perfect blue. A jagged crack had formed as one would expect to see in a wall after an earthquake, its edges sharp enough to cut anyone who dared to touch them. Natalia gasped as she realized that the crack was big enough to see *through*… to the other side.

The image in the crack was dark and foreboding. A desolate, lifeless mass of gray concrete that loomed on the other side. There was nothing to the image, no personality, no character, just this blank gray face, as though the city in the sky felt nothing at all.

"Raziel," Natalia whispered, her fingers gripping the balcony railing so tightly that the stone shattered beneath her grasp.

If anything was the embodiment of her sister, it was that city. The barrier between their worlds was beginning to crumble, her powers failing. She needed to fix things before the barrier fell completely, and her world collided with that of her sister's. She would *not* be the one to fail!

Natalia hurried into the bathroom, shedding her robe the moment she stepped into the room. She didn't care that John was there; it wasn't as if she'd ever been ashamed of her body, and she wasn't about to start now. She *should* have been amused, or even satisfied, by the way John blushed and looked away from her naked frame, but instead, she felt nothing at all. Natalia could feel every beat of her heart, her chest aching as though it were a foreign object that didn't belong there. It was the only thing she *could* feel at this point; everything else felt numb, empty, lifeless.

She stood at the edge of the bath for a moment and stared at her reflection as it wavered in the water. Even *she* was beginning to lose her shine. She'd never looked so dull, so tired and washed out before. The shimmering curls she loved so much seemed muddier and thinner than usual, though she was sure it was all her imagination. Not to mention, her usually stunning blue eyes seemed pale and tired. Never in her life would she have believed that she could look so plain.

"I'm not sure this vase would shine even if it *were* cracked," Natalia hissed, kicking the surface of the water with her foot, dismissing her own image as she slid into the warm water until she slipped into its depths.

Natalia was aware of Helena pacing alongside the edge of the bath while she remained beneath the water, the bubbles spreading themselves out again now that the bath had settled and the ripples vanished. For a minute, Natalia wasn't sure she *wanted* to resurface, or whether she would rather drown in the warm embrace of the bathwater.

At least she felt *something* while she was in there, which was more than she'd really felt in the last few… hours? Days? Weeks? She couldn't tell the passage of time anymore, and she couldn't say with any certainty how long any of this had been happening.

A strong pair of hands broke the calm surface of the water, grasping at her wet, naked body. Before Natalia could protest or push the hands away, she was wrenched from the depths of the water and dragged to the surface, where she found herself face-to-face with John. He stared into her eyes with a scowl on his face, and she wondered why he wore that expression at all. Surely, all of his troubles would be over if she were dead. So, why did he care if she drowned or not?

"Are you alright?" he asked.

"Why do you care?" she asked in return. "Have you suddenly had a change of heart? You've seen me naked and decided that you want me, just like all those who came before you?"

John sighed heavily, his tight grip on her upper arms shifting to a gentler pressure on her shoulders as he sat at the edge of the bath beside her. His eyes never left hers, in a way that was a complete opposite to how Jules had been with her. What color had Jules' eyes been? She couldn't remember because he'd never been able to look at her for any length of time, and she'd never thought anything of it until now.

"I care, in my way. You've changed, whether you want to admit it or not, and you're willing to give us all a better life. You don't get the easy way out. Living is your reward as much as your punishment. A do-over on the world you want to rule while being forced to *learn* from the error of your ways. You lost the man you loved, and you have to live with that, but you get to start again, and maybe this time, you'll find someone who sees something in you the way he clearly did."

Natalia looked away from him, scowling as he used Jules against her.

"Tell me about the woman you love. Tell me why you fell in love with her."

"Sophie?" John raised an eyebrow at her and smiled softly, looking at Helena for a moment before he looked away wistfully. "She loves to paint; it was the first thing I noticed about her. I saw her sneak out one night, by one of your fountains, to paint the city beneath the night sky. She looked happy, *truly* happy, as though she didn't have a care in the world. I wondered how anyone could look so content when I felt as though I was filled with this suffocating darkness. How could she *still* love painting when you forced us to constantly give you gifts of your image? Yet, she didn't seem to care so long as she was painting. I asked her about it once, and she said she could lose herself in her paintings, that each brushstroke was *her* choice. It was her way of keeping control in a world where we didn't have any control in what we could or could not do. I never realized I could love anyone the way I loved her."

Natalia leaned on the side of the bath, listening intently to each word while Helena ran a sponge over her skin. She could see the priestess watching *her* rather than John, clearly interested in her reaction to the rebel's words.

"John, will you take a message to the rest of the city? Tell them that I want to speak to them tomorrow. We will start over, a new world, where they can have more control of their lives while still worshipping me. I want to see what you see in the world. Maybe then, I can appreciate my own strengths even more than I do now."

"Is that even remotely possible?" John chuckled.

Natalia rolled her eyes at him and smiled softly. John threw his arms in the air and cheered, causing Helena to jump with shock.

"She smiles!" He laughed.

"On occasion. Will you do it?" she asked again.

"I will. Though, don't start thinking that I'm going to be

your new Head Priest. No way am I going to be replacing Jules." He snorted.

"As if you could," Natalia replied, standing up, smirking as John averted his gaze with a hand rather than staring at her naked, wet body. "No one can replace him," she added softly as she stepped out of the tub, wrapping the robe that Helena offered her around her body.

"Go on, Helena will help you get back out into the city. Tell the rebels to stop their assault on the palace, and we will talk tomorrow. I want one last night before I have to stand before them."

John nodded and stood up with a smile on his face. "I will, and I think they will be more than happy to listen, considering you're offering them a chance at a *new* utopia. A proper one."

Natalia smiled in return, glancing at Helena. She wondered what the woman thought of all of this. Not just the potentially new direction their lives would take, but also the fact that she had so blatantly admitted to loving Jules. Helena *said* she loved Natalia, and she had no reason to lie about it, considering she could easily have joined the rebellion at the doors of the palace if she wanted to.

Natalia was grateful—something she'd never been before —for Helena's loyalty and devotion, but she didn't feel that way about the woman. She couldn't imagine her life without the priestess, but it wasn't the same feeling that she felt about Jules. Now that she could admit that, she felt that she understood herself a little better as well.

She'd lost Jules before she'd found him. Raziel had spent her entire *life* looking for love, unable to understand it, let alone feel it, and Natalia had lost love before she'd even realized she had it all along. All because she hadn't realized she needed it in that way, let alone that she was even capable of loving someone other than herself.

His absence from her side left her cold, and she wasn't sure if she would ever get used to it, but for now, she might be able to salvage the mess that she was in and reach a point where her citizens loved her again... truly loved her this time.

Natalia spent her evening staring up at the scar in the sky that hung over the city. She'd heard the acolytes and priestesses whispering about it on her return to her bedroom, and chose to ignore them when one of the priestesses hurried over to whisper in Helena's ear about it. They were less subtle than they all thought they were. Either that, or Natalia was more aware of their gossiping now because she was purposefully *not* talking about it.

She looked back at her Head Priestess, and the moment they made eye contact, she knew Helena wouldn't bother to ask her about the situation. If *she* didn't bring it up, it was best not to.

Natalia raised a hand to the sky, wiggling her fingers at the city that sat where Heaven, technically, should be. It felt as though she could touch the buildings if she stretched her arm enough. Her sister's world was so close, yet still so far away.

"Do you miss us?" Raziel asked, and Natalia imagined her sister staring up at the same scar, only seeing Natalia's bright, gleaming world.

They were almost polar opposites of one another. She'd always known that, but seeing Raziel's world lingering just out of reach while her sister could see *hers*, she realized just how different they were. She was all sunshine and golden city, while her sister's world was bleak and gray. What was it like to live life feeling... well... nothing?

"*Miss* is a strong word." Natalia chuckled as she sat back on her hands, staring at the dim glowing lights in her sibling's city skyscrapers. "I don't know. I'm beginning to see things a little differently, that's all," Natalia admitted, pressing on the boundaries of her mind to see if she could feel Azazel lurking in the shadows, ready to tease her. Thankfully, it seemed their other sister was occupied elsewhere, and there wasn't even the slightest inkling of her presence anywhere to be felt.

"Your humans really have changed you, haven't they?"

"I'd like to think of it as growth, if you don't mind." Natalia snorted. "I'm merely finding new ways of being even better than I am already, not that I really needed to improve. Perfect as I am."

"And yet, here we are, discussing how you've begun to learn despite being flawless."

"Let me ask you this, Sister. Have you changed since we last met?" Natalia snapped, not so content with allowing her sister to think that only Natalia was changing while their worlds also crumbled around them.

"Maybe. Though I couldn't tell you how. You know my search just as well as I do, yet I do not feel as though I am any closer to understanding it. I don't feel as you and Azazel do. Beyond frustrated that I don't feel at all, I suppose. Frustration is about as close as I can get to a true emotion, and it's not the one I seek."

"Pathetic."

It never ceased to amaze Natalia that Azazel could say one word and convey a multitude of emotions all at once. Self-satisfied, disgusted, amused. All balled into one word spat across their steadily strengthening connection. Azazel could deny what was happening all she wanted, but the siblings were in communication more in recent days than they had been in centuries. What other explanation could she give beyond the fact that their powers were waning?

"And to think I once considered the two of you my equals, if not my rivals," she continued snidely. "Weaklings, that's what you both are. Pathetic excuses for angels that I cannot believe I ever thought could go up against me. You're no rivals of mine."

"Your betters, I think you'll find," Natalia replied, closing her eyes as she gathered all of her strength and cast her sister from her mind.

She groaned as she felt Azazel's presence thrown from her mind, her body slumping on the balcony and threatening to topple into the street below as all her strength left her at once.

"It won't be long before we cannot ignore one another," Raziel whispered, her own voice distant and weak.

"I know. But I've not given up yet. I told you, I'm growing and learning new ways to be better than both of you. Soon, I will wipe your foul city from my sky *and* from my mind, and

I will sever our connection permanently, *proving* that I am the best of us. You'll see," Natalia hissed, stumbling from the balcony and turning her back on the strange city that mocked her with its existence in her world.

Tomorrow.

Tomorrow, things would change forever, and no one, not even God, would be able to deny her power.

Natalia awoke bright and early the next day, rejuvenated from both sleep and a renewed confidence in herself. It wasn't that she had grown weaker; she'd just gotten lazy. She knew that now. John had pointed out that there was more than just the superficial beauty she'd been obsessed with. There was an inner beauty, something that appeared even stronger than she could ever have imagined.

She would *always* be the most beautiful woman in the entire Universe, but what if people could come to love her for that as *well* as her ambition, her courage, her strength of character? She would be unstoppable. God really wouldn't be able to shy away from her powers and grace then.

The palace shone a little brighter, her powers radiating from her. She *knew* she was stronger and more powerful than her sisters would have her believe. It was only her doubt that had caused her power to waver, and now that she *knew* that, everything would return to normal!

Natalia all but skipped her way down the glistening corridors of her palace to the main Throne Room, ready to greet her citizens with renewed vigor. Even the scar in the sky couldn't dampen her spirits today. Soon, it would be a distant memory, a foul taste in her mouth that would be easily forgotten with the sweet taste of victory that she would soon be consuming. Today was a new day, and it was the beginning of her crowning glory.

Before long, she would be rid of the dark shadow that still gripped her stomach and twisted it. Azazel's words still stung more than Natalia liked to admit, but she was about to prove her howling sister wrong in *everything* that Azazel had ever said to her. Soon, Natalia wouldn't have to think about her sister, let alone suffer listening to her voice.

No. Today was her day, and today, she would be rid of her past once and for all.

N atalia strode across her Throne Room, dark curls cascading over her back, her reflection grinning at her happily as Helena fell into step behind her. Soon, the acolytes and priestesses followed suit, their footsteps soft as they hurried along behind their Mistress, sharing worried and nervous looks that Natalia could see out of the corner of her eye.

She knew they weren't sure about pulling down the barricade and inviting the rebels to their door unguarded, but Natalia knew she could win them over again. John had gone out into the world on her behalf to speak to the rebels, he'd spent time with her, and she *supposed* he could boast that he had opened her eyes to the new possibilities within herself. He would tell the others that she was going to redo everything, that they would have a new chance at life under her guidance. She could better them, shape them more into her image, show them how to become better versions of themselves, and in return, she would get to show them her *inner* self.

With a wave of her hands, the acolytes pulled down the last of the barricade, casting it aside with uneasy looks before they grasped the handles of the main doors and wrenched them open. Sunlight poured across the polished surface of the golden floors for the first time since they had been forced to shut them against the city.

Natalia smiled as the sun warmed her bare feet and legs, its rays rushing to embrace her silken skin with its comforting embrace. Stepping out of the palace and onto the steps, Natalia spread her arms wide as though inviting her citizens to embrace *her*. She'd expected cheers of joy at her reunion with her citizens, but instead, she was met with silence. For a brief second, Natalia faltered, hesitating before she took another step toward the crowd gathered in front of the building.

Her eyes scanned the faces before her, and Natalia spotted John at the front of them, nodding his own silent encouragement to her. Just as she hadn't realized how much she would miss Jules, Natalia was surprised to find herself glad to see the man there at that moment. He had come to bask in her glory, but she also felt encouraged to do this because he was there.

Natalia nodded to him in return, amused when the pretty woman beside him stared at him in shock. Clearly, she was *the* Sophie he'd spoken about before, and Natalia had a vague recollection of the woman offering her gifts on the days when her citizens had given their tithes.

"My citizens!" Natalia proudly called to them all, her arms still spread wide to signify her welcoming them back into the fold. "I know that my envoy, John, has sent you my message. I am here to tell you that it is indeed true; we are going to build a better world. Together. Yes, I still expect you to worship me, to understand that it is by *my* grace that you'll still live in my personally-made utopia. However, I will not enforce the tithe as I did previously, nor will I stop you from exploring relationships with one another. Just remember that this is *my* gift to you. That you are saved from the heartache and pain that my sisters, or even my *father*, would have put you through."

She glanced at John, who rolled his eyes at her a little but still smiled. She'd told him she couldn't change who she was, nor would she want to; she was perfect. She might be willing to learn, but that didn't mean she was going to stop being true to herself. She was just going to be a better version of herself.

The citizens glanced at one another and began to mutter amongst themselves as they began to discuss what she'd said. She could tell they weren't convinced, and some were clearly still looking to fight back against her, but Natalia watched as John began to put their minds at ease. She couldn't hear him, but she could see that he was mitigating any hostilities from the others.

There was a rumble of agreement through the crowd, a hushed sense of positivity that steadily grew into a crescendo of excited chatter. Natalia smiled as John caught her eye and gave her a quick thumbs up. She had won back her people, and clearly, they were ready to try again.

They knew how easy they had it with her. She was far kinder than any of her siblings would have been, let alone the suffering that God would have put them through. Finally, it was time for them to learn and grow together again.

"Pathetic, weak excuse for an angel. You call yourself a goddess, and yet here you are, bending your will to these creatures? They are insects meant to be crushed beneath our boots, and yet you compromise with them? I knew you were weaker than me; I knew I was the best of all of us, not you. All your bravado, all your ego, and you let them manipulate you."

Azazel's words stung. Her sister knew how to rile her; she always had, telling her that she was weaker than these humans she was *supposedly* above. No, she was above *them*; she was the one in charge here… That doubt that she thought she'd shaken off began to creep back in, icy fingers of disbelief that she could be anything other than almighty gripping her heart.

"No," she whispered, shaking her head as though dismissing her sister from her mind. "NO!" The word roared across the city, causing the ground to shake violently, bricks cascading from the buildings as they crumbled under the force of the shockwaves.

"This is *my* world! I created it with my own two hands, and I will *not* be manipulated by pathetic insects like *you*. You *will* love me; you *will* respect me. You will bow at my feet, kiss my toes, and be *grateful for the fact that you are allowed to live in this paradise!*" Natalia's shrill tone cut through the city like a scythe.

The buildings around her shuddered as her voice hit them. They stood tall for a moment, as proud as they ever had, before their tops sheared from the lower levels and crashed into the streets below. The citizens screamed in fear, scattering as the buildings collapsed around them.

Natalia stared at her reflection by her feet, sneering angrily at the black-eyed woman staring back at her as a red mist began to descend over her.

Pain lanced through every part of her body as she writhed and twisted against the changes in her body. The dark shadow of doubt had been replaced by a raging fire of fury, the inferno burning her from within. She watched herself changing in the reflective walls of the palace.

Her perfect ivory skin stretched and tore, great gashes of angry red and thick black scales forming where smooth skin had been once before. Her beautiful curls became lank and even darker, sickly black like thick strands of oil made solid, matching her hollow eyes that seemed to glow red with the fire growing within herself. Her back twitched and convulsed, her bones cracking audibly as huge leathery wings sprouted from between her shoulder blades. All her beauty was gone, replaced with the dark horror that sprouted from the doubt and hatred she now felt so strongly.

Natalia's mind thought of only one thing—shredding these pathetic insects apart with her new claws, tearing their flesh with her new fangs, and tasting their blood on her serpent-like tongue. They would pay; they would *all* pay.

Stretching her new wings, Natalia threw back her head and screamed with a mixture of elation and anger. She felt powerful; she felt *strong*. A growling laugh escaped her throat, and Natalia turned on the citizens screaming and shouting to get as far away as possible from the horror that she had become. There was no saving them now. All they'd had to do was love her, but that had been too much to ask, and now, she would destroy them.

Raising her scaled fists above her head, Natalia brought them down as hard as she could upon the ground. The shockwaves shuddered out like ripples on water, and her citizens struggled to keep on their feet, most of them collapsing to the ground, covering their heads with their arms against the falling debris from the buildings. She would destroy them; she would see them *all* suffer.

Natalia flapped her wings, growling happily at the feeling of the air as it moved around them. Oh, how she had missed being able to fly, that sweet feeling of freedom that she just didn't get from anything else. The wind rushed to embrace her as the sky turned black to match her heart. Clouds gathered in the sky for the first time since she had created her world, blocking Raziel's city from view. Thunder rumbled like the drums of war, a herald of the hell she intended to rain down upon the insects that dared to insult her, while lightning flashed bright and terrible in the darkness, splitting the sky in two.

They would bow. They would kneel. She would show them *all*. Natalia closed her eyes and raised her hands to Heaven, wings sweeping through the air with ease as though she had never been without them. A dark power gathered inside her, terrible and new as it filled every fiber of her being, tickling her nerves with electricity. Her forked tongue flickered over her lips as she tasted the raw power in the very air around her.

She gathered it to her, drawing it into herself and focusing all of that natural potential into her fingertips to create a pool of it in her palms. She visualized the flames in her heart, pulling them out into the air until they manifested in her hands, their warmth flickering and licking at her skin.

She then opened her eyes and let out a mirthless laugh, the sound grating, lightyears from the melodic laughter she'd known all her life to be her own. She looked at the balls of fire she had summoned and smiled, her fangs pricking her bottom lip. She flicked her wrists, fire cascading to the ground below, raining down from the thick black clouds that had gathered above her.

Screams echoed from the streets, panic and fear palpable in the air, sweeter than she could ever have imagined. All they had to do was love her, and they could have avoided all of this; now, she would see them writhe in pain.

Natalia descended from her vantage point, landing gracefully before the entrance to her palace. She cocked her head to one side, grinning maliciously as she watched her citizens collide with one another, pushing each other out of the way in an attempt to save themselves from the fireballs raining down upon them.

The stench of charred flesh and smoke filled the air, acrid and suffocating. Yet Natalia breathed deeply, savoring each taste of it on her tongue as she filled her lungs with it. The ground cracked, and she watched gleefully as several citizens were swallowed whole by the earth.

"My Lady! *Please*, stop this!" Helena's voice begged above the cacophony of wails and cries that filled the air.

Natalia felt a pressure on her arm, and she turned her head toward it slowly, hissing at the hand that she found wrapped around her wrist. Her head whipped around, and she bared her fangs at her priestess. Helena leapt backwards, eyes wide, her fear written all over her face. Natalia grinned maliciously, stepping toward the priestess threateningly.

"Stop it! Just stop this!" another voice screamed at her, and Natalia spun around to face the person who *dared* to believe they could stop her from doing what she wanted.

Even in her rage-fueled state, Natalia recognized the face of the woman who had saved Helena from her wrath. Sophie. The woman whom John had *dared* fall in love with when all of his attention *should* have been on Natalia.

Natalia hissed angrily, her wings quivering on her back as she lowered her body, claws extended as all her attention focused on the woman.

She could see the fear in Sophie's eyes as she realized what was about to happen, Natalia's body trembling like a coiled spring. A predator ready to pounce upon its prey, fangs primed to tear out the throat of the woman frozen before her. A deer facing a lioness. With a scream of rage, Natalia launched herself at the woman, ready to strike her down and taste her blood.

Sophie didn't move, her fear causing her to freeze in place. Natalia raised her claws, ready to slash the woman's pretty face, wanting to feel her flesh distort and twist. She wouldn't be beautiful ever again; Natalia would make sure of that. The space between them closed, and Natalia let out a shriek of joy as she anticipated the satisfactory feeling of flesh tearing under her claws.

Suddenly, there was movement out of the corner of her eye. Before Natalia could stop herself or do anything else, John pushed Sophie out of the way and bore the brunt of Natalia's wrath himself. She felt her claws rake through skin, muscle, and bone, like metal grating on rock. His blood poured over her hands, warm and sticky.

Natalia stumbled, collapsing to her knees beside his fallen body, her hand trembling as John's blood dripped from her scales. She stared at the mangled mess that had been the man's face, his body convulsing as he gasped for air, gurgling as he choked and drowned in his own blood.

"Why?" She gasped, staring at his one remaining eye. "*Why?!*"

"Because I love her!" He gasped also, reaching out a hand to Natalia, his body quaking with the effort. "Be better," he whispered as he grasped her hand in his, his fingers squeezing her hand for a moment before he went limp.

"John?" Natalia whispered, placing a hand upon his chest and shaking him lightly.

She could feel his heartbeat, faint and growing weaker by the second, but it was there. Natalia stared at her hand on his chest, her eyes drawn to Sophie who stood close by, wailing at the sight of her lover in this state. Natalia cocked her head to one side slightly. She could not hear anything, not even the terrible grieving shriek of the woman, and she realized that the world had fallen silent for her.

He'd given his life for the woman he loved, just as Jules had for her when she'd been assaulted. He was willing to die for Sophie, and yet he *still* wanted Natalia to know that she could do better. Why did he care? Why did he make that effort even after all of this? She'd hurt him badly; she'd killed the others, and he still wanted her to know that he believed in her.

He truly loved Sophie, just as Jules had loved her. Her sisters, her family, none of them would have ever given their lives in the way that John and Jules had. They'd sacrificed themselves for love, a love that Natalia had wanted all her life but never really understood. She'd been determined for these people to love her, but what had she ever done to deserve it? Why had Jules given his life for her? Why would John *still* care enough to use his last breath to encourage her to improve?

Natalia's hand gripped John's blood-covered shirt, feeling the ever-slowing heartbeat in his chest. Her heart ached for what she had done, for hurting someone who had stood up to her and *dared* to tell her that she could be more than she already was. Tears blurred her vision as she clung to his body, oblivious to the continuing destruction around them as she focused solely on him.

No. She wasn't going to lose him like she'd lost Jules. She needed him to show her the way, to help her find her *inner* light so that she might one day find love again. She wanted to find someone who could love her as Jules had, someone she could share her life with.

"I can do better. I can be better. I *am better*. And I'm going to prove it to you," Natalia growled, shifting her weight onto her knees as she pressed both her palms to John's chest.

Even now, she could feel that her powers were different—not weaker as such, just new and unfamiliar. Closing her eyes, Natalia took in a slow, deep breath. She could feel the raw power she'd tapped into before, when she'd first transformed into a demon, but she dismissed it. That raw power was full of anger and hate, and that wasn't her; that wasn't *her* strength. Healing wasn't exactly her specialty; it wasn't what God had designed her to do, but all angels had some form of healing powers. Latent and lingering under the surface.

"What are you doing to him?!" Sophie hissed at her, breaking her concentration.

"Saving his life. Do you want to *help* or just get in my way?" Natalia hissed in return, opening her eyes and gasping as her reflection stared back at her from Sophie's large brown eyes.

The black scales were receding, the slick strands of hair dripped their oil onto John's almost lifeless body, her shiny curls glistening beneath. It wasn't any of this that shocked her; it was her wings. When she had fallen, God took her wings as part of her punishment, but as the leathery skin shed away, it revealed the bright white feathers that she had known all her life. Restored to their former glory, gleaming with the light of the stars above.

Sophie placed a hand on Natalia's, the other on John's disfigured face. Natalia felt Sophie's love for John, and her acceptance—and maybe even an ounce of gratitude—toward Natalia for what she was about to do. Focusing on that energy, on the love the citizens around her had for one another and the man lying on the ground, Natalia felt the warmth grow beneath her fingers moments before the golden glow appeared.

She let the healing energy gather at her fingertips before she pumped John's chest with her palms, forcing the energy and light directly into his body. The bleeding stopped in John's wounds, and the gashes healed for the most part, even though Natalia felt herself unable to completely rid him of the scar tissue that she had unfortunately gifted him.

Natalia panted heavily, beads of sweat gathering on her

forehead as she focused her energy on bringing John's body back from the brink. His body convulsed beneath her hands, and Natalia fell back, gasping for breath in unison with John. He sat up sharply, blinking in confusion as he looked at his lover, bawling against his rising and falling chest, to the smug-looking—if somewhat exhausted—angel beside him.

"You saved my life," he croaked.

"Sadly, I didn't have the strength to save your face." She snorted in return, one hand on her chest as she winced at the steady burn of her lungs.

"Inner beauty." John chuckled, tapping his face and grimacing a little at the pain that still lingered there. "Why?"

"You reminded me of Jules. Of the sacrifice he made for me, and why I'd promised to make this world anew." She sighed, struggling to her feet.

Natalia stumbled and gasped as she felt the world give way beneath her feet, but rather than the cold hard ground rushing to meet her, Natalia found herself bolstered by the crowds. Men and women rushed to embrace her, catching her as she fell and supporting her. Lending her their strength.

She stared at them all. Their faces covered in burn marks and soot, bloody and bruised from head to toe, and *still* willing to stand there and help her after all that she had done.

"Be better," John whispered, tapping his scarred face again with a flinch, his remaining good eye beaming at her as he smiled.

Natalia smiled and nodded in return to him. She'd been naïve. She was strong, and she may be the strongest being in the world, but that didn't mean she was infallible. Even God had needed his angels, so why had she ever believed that she could be any different?

Was this what you meant about me learning a lesson? she asked Him silently, glancing up at the renewed blue skies, and Raziel's city sat within the scar, wondering if her father was smiling down on her from His own throne.

N atalia gently shook her people from herself, offering a small smile to them to show that she would be alright, and that they had her thanks. She could see the looks of mistrust and surprise, and for once, she didn't blame them. Her anger, her doubt in herself, had all led to her becoming a demon. They'd all discussed the possibilities and reasons why angels twisted into Hell spawns, but there had never been any definitive proof. Most of the fallen were just that, fallen, not mindless demons hell-bent on bloodthirsty destruction.

"All of you, stand together on the steps. Helena, I'm sorry

for frightening you. Can you clear the palace for me?" she asked.

The priestess hesitated for a minute, huddled amongst a group of other shivering priestesses and acolytes who looked equal parts confused and scared. Natalia reached around to her newly-formed wings and plucked one of her glistening feathers from the limb, wincing at the sharp pain and sighing as a spot of blood began to form and filter into the feathers below. There was an ache in her heart at the imperfection, but that was also part of the point. Natalia held the feather out to her priestess as she moved toward her slowly, her free hand up to show that she meant no harm.

Helena held out a hand, unable to stop herself from shaking, but still willing to try. Natalia placed her feather onto the woman's outstretched palm, cupping Helena's hand with hers and curling the priestess' fingers around the feather.

"Once you have everyone, make sure you all hold hands and think of me. The feather will bring you straight back here," Natalia whispered. "It will also keep you safe from any potential falling debris. Be safe, but be quick."

Helena nodded and hurried into the palace, gripping the feather as she vanished through the crooked main doors and into the crumbling building that had once stood so tall and proud.

An hour passed before Helena reappeared on the palace steps with the remaining priestesses and acolytes who had taken shelter in the palace while Natalia was losing her mind to the darkness. They looked uncertainly at their Mistress as Natalia ushered them onto the steps with the rest of her people, squishing them all together.

"What are you up to?" John asked, raising an eyebrow at her, his face struggling with the movement as the scar tissue stretched uncomfortably.

Natalia stared at the man for a moment, taking in his scarred face, the scars that *she* had caused. His right eye would never recover, and while the red raw flesh would eventually settle and become less uncomfortable for the man, they would never fade. An ugly reminder of the day she'd lost herself, almost completely. It was strange, as not so long ago, Natalia would have been repulsed at the very sight of him. Yet now, when she looked at the huge red marks that marred his once handsome face, Natalia didn't see an ugly man at all.

She reached a hand out to the man, gently touching his cheek and tracing a finger over one of the scars that she'd given him with a smile on her face. "Light shines through a cracked vase."

John laughed, immediately grimacing as his face stretched, rolling his eyes at her. "Fuck you, too." He snorted.

Grinning, Natalia gently moved him behind her with her wings. She spread her arms wide and took a deep breath. The wind whipped around them all, causing several members of the crowd to gasp in surprise as bits of debris were gathered by the air, spinning above their heads.

"Watch this," Natalia said smugly, loud enough for John to hear her over the roaring gale she seemingly commanded now.

The world crumbled around them, and she vaguely heard people screaming behind her, though their voices were snatched away by the wind and whipped away from her ears. The palace crumbled alongside the city, leaving only the steps and courtyard where her citizens had gathered for safety. Natalia could already feel her body aching, straining against any further use of her powers, but she had promised her people a new world, and she would give them just that.

A new city grew around them, still glistening gold, bright and shining. The wind grew quiet, and Natalia lowered her hands with a gasp, her knees buckling beneath her. John and Helena rushed to catch her, and Natalia smiled softly.

"Thank you," she muttered.

"What did you do?" Helena asked, scowling at her.

"I created a new world. For all of us," she replied.

"What?"

"Go and look; see for yourselves." Natalia chuckled, standing upright and brushing at her tattered clothes, trying not to weep at the state she must be in. "I promised you all a fresh start, and I almost killed you all, so I've made this world anew. Now we can *really* start over, all of us. I just hope, someday, that might include some *others* who aren't here right now," she added, glancing up at Raziel's world, peering through the scar in the sky.

Her citizens began to scatter, hurrying to see the changes that had been made, feeling more at ease that Natalia was being true to her word this time. Natalia smiled at John and Sophie, furling her wings against her back as she strode confidently into her renewed palace.

On the surface, it looked as though nothing had changed. Everything was still gold, the surfaces polished into glistening mirrors so that she could see her reflection with every turn of her head. Entering the Throne Room, Natalia turned her head to watch as John, Sophie, and Helena all entered. They gasped collectively at the sight, leaving Natalia grinning widely.

"What do you think?" she asked, waving a hand at the new palace with a flourish.

Surrounding her throne was a grand statue of herself, her newly-formed wings spread wide to embrace the men and women who stood beside her, all of whom were looking up at her adoringly. The walls were, for once, not reflective at all, covered in a variety of murals depicting Natalia engaged in a variety of activities with the men and women she called her citizens. From playing music together, to painting, to strolling through the forests or splashing in the rivers.

The central mural didn't depict Natalia at all. Jules' image dominated the wall, a serene expression on his face, a halo glowing around his head as though he had been given his sainthood.

As Natalia's eyes settled on the image, she smiled sadly, her heart twinging as she felt the loss of him again. He would never see this new world, this new start, but she still wanted him to be a part of it in some way. If it hadn't been for Jules and John, Natalia would never have started to understand love.

This was her way of thanking him.

"I thought it was going to be *less* about you." John snorted, chuckling as he motioned to the images on the wall.

"What?! They're not *all* me, are they?" she asked, pointing to Jules' image with a look that said, "argue with that."

"One out of how many?" John laughed.

"I've got other citizens in the images, too. It's not like I'm the *only* image now. And I've got you down perfectly." She smirked, pointing to the statue by her throne where John stood beside her, and then to a mural where he was rolling his eyes at her.

"Yeah, I can't argue there." He exhaled.

"I told you. I can't change my nature. I might be able to learn, but I'm always going to be myself." Natalia chuckled, crossing her arms over her chest.

She might have learnt a little more about herself, and she might be willing to learn more about herself and the people around her, but she still knew she was the most beautiful being in the Universe, and she was also the strongest. She couldn't have believed anything other than that. She knew what she was capable of, and she had proven her prowess in rebuilding her world all over again. She'd always known she was amazing; now no one else could deny it, either.

"So, what now?" John asked, hugging Sophie to his side.

"We live. In the way we should have done when I first created this world. I will help all of you become better versions of yourself, more in my image as I should have done before, and you will teach me to see the value of a person from *within*. Not just by their looks."

John chuckled and glanced at Helena for a moment. Natalia looked at the priestess, too, watching as the woman took in the new sites that surrounded her, clearly trying to work out where she fitted into this new world that Natalia had created.

"I hope my sisters can join us one day, but for now, we can learn and grow together." Natalia shrugged, striding back out of the palace.

She turned to face the scar where her sister's city laid, reaching a hand toward the dark, emotionless place as though she could pluck it from the sky and bring it closer. Their powers were growing weaker, but only because they needed to learn to be better versions of themselves. Natalia wondered what lesson her sisters were learning beyond the barrier, and whether they would learn it at all or be destroyed as she almost had been.

"Look! Another scar in the sky!" Helena gasped as she

joined Natalia outside the palace, pointing to a place opposite the scar where Raziel's city lingered.

It was new, and not quite opened yet, not enough to see the world beyond. Natalia could see vague shapes in the bright white tear, and knew that Azazel lurked in the space beyond. So much for her sister being the *better* of them. It seemed even she could not deny her failings now, not when the barrier was beginning to crumble between their two worlds.

Soon, their worlds would collide, and they would all be together again, unless her sisters fell to their own citizens first, or to the darkness lingering in their own hearts. Natalia rubbed at her chest, feeling the remnants of that dark shadow that had almost consumed her, twisting her body beyond recognition.

Natalia managed to compose herself, stopping herself from shuddering as she remembered the ugly, twisted creature she'd become. Was that the ugliness that John had accused her of having inside? If so, she wasn't sure she ever wanted to see *that* again.

Natalia looked from one scar to the other, smiling softly to herself. Her sisters were closer to her than they had been in centuries. She wished Jules were still with her, but she could learn to love again; she was sure of that. He'd opened her heart to the possibility, showing Natalia that she was capable of loving someone *other* than herself. Even John held a special place in her heart now, which felt oddly comforting. Natalia looked at Helena and smiled, wondering what the woman would become to her now.

Whatever the future held, she was walking new ground. Becoming an even *better* version of her perfect self, and no one would be able to deny how glorious she truly was.

To be continued...

ABOUT THE AUTHOR

Viola Tempest is a dystopian fantasy and paranormal romance author who yearns to expose the truth of those in the modern world: the good, the bad, and the ugly. Her inspiration primarily stems from life experiences, those who annoy her, ex-boyfriends, and the crazy dreams that pop into her head every once in a while.